KU-463-633

STEPHEN GREGORY

The author was born in Derby in 1952 and graduated in law from London University in 1973. After eleven years in various teaching jobs, including stints in Algiers and Sudan, he decided to go and live in a remote cottage in North Wales in order to write full-time. He has had short stories published in *The Illustrated London News* and the *Anglo-Welsh Review*. THE CORMORANT is his first novel.

sceptre

'An air of menace that builds slowly, unremittingly towards an explosive climax. This is a short novel, told throughout in a direct, unadorned prose that maintains a relentless forward drive and creates an air of credibility. A simple tale straightforwardly told, but keeping in check the violence and the slight drift towards the macabre only makes it the more powerful. Stephen Gregory's first novel is a work of tremendous self-assurance that leaves the reader with a lingering sense of unease, and announces the arrival of a considerable new talent'

British Book News

'After reading this book it is easy to see why Milton characterised Satan as a cormorant'

The Literary Review

Stephen Gregory

THE CORMORANT

For my Mother and Father

Copyright © Stephen Gregory 1986

First published in Great Britain in 1986 by William Heinemann Ltd.

Sceptre edition 1987
Second impression 1987

This book is sold subject to the condition that it shall not, by way of trade or otherwise, be lent, re-sold, hired out or otherwise circulated without the publisher's prior consent in any form of binding or cover other than that in which this is published and without a similar condition including this condition being imposed on the subsequent purchaser.

Sceptre is an imprint of Hodder and Stoughton Paperbacks, a division of Hodder and Stoughton Ltd.

British Library C.I.P.

Gregory, Stephen
  The cormorant.
  I. Title
  823'.914[F]   PR6057.R38/

  ISBN 0-340-41690-4

Printed and bound in Great Britain for Hodder and Stoughton Paperbacks, a division of Hodder and Stoughton Ltd., Mill Road, Dunton Green, Sevenoaks, Kent (Editorial Office: 47 Bedford Square, London, WC1B 3DP) by Richard Clay Ltd., Bungay, Suffolk. Photoset by Rowland Phototypesetting Ltd., Bury St Edmunds, Suffolk.

ONE

The crate was delivered to the cottage at five o'clock in the afternoon. Two men carried it into our little living-room, put it down in front of the fire, and then they drove away in their van. For the next four hours, I left it there and continued working at my desk. I built up the fire with coal and a few freshly-split logs of spruce from the forest, cooked some supper, leaving some to stay warm for my wife until she came in from working in the village. Outside, it grew dark and there was the pattering of fine rain on the windows of the cottage. The wind blew up and made the trees of the plantation rattle. It was October. I could hear the tumbling of the stream at the foot of the garden, a reassuring sound, a background to the explosive crackle of the logs, the whining of wet wood in the growing heat of the fire. A curtain of drizzle concealed the mountains, they were dissolved into the sky, removed from around the village as though they had never been there. I worked for a while and I ate. The crate stood silent on the rug, in front of the hearth.

It was a box of white wood, about three feet square, with a panel of perforations on the top to ventilate the contents. Once or twice, in the course of the evening, I got up from the desk, knelt by the crate and sniffed at the tiny holes. I blew into them. I smelt the new wood, its clean, useful smell, and from the perforations there came the pungent whiff of the beach, the rotten air of an estuary which dries a little and sweats before the return of the cleansing tide. Inside the box, there was something warm and breathing, asleep perhaps, sleeping in a bed of stale straw. No sound, no movement. I returned to my work, but I was restless so I abandoned it for another look at the newspaper. Sometimes, as I read, my hand strayed and rested on the corner of the white wooden crate. When my wife came in at nine o'clock we would open it together.

Ann went immediately upstairs to take off her wet clothes and to inspect the baby. I could hear her shaking her coat, and imagined the shower of raindrops against the mirror in the bedroom as she dried her thick, brown hair with a towel. She went to the tiny back room and found the baby sound asleep; I had been up to check that he was all right each time I left my desk, my paper and the crate. She came down again, her cheeks pink with her efforts on the bicycle through the enveloping darkness and with the business of drying her hair. She was carrying the cat by the scruff of its neck.

'Don't let the cat go upstairs when Harry's in bed,' she said, dropping the animal unceremoniously onto the sofa. 'It was curled up on his pillow. Otherwise, my love,' and she presented her cheek for me to kiss, 'everything seems to be in order. Good boy.'

The cat leapt across the room and sniffed at the box. It arched its back, rubbed itself luxuriously on the corners of the crate.

'So,' said Ann. 'It's arrived. Let's open it and see what we've got.'

The fire was burning quickly in the grate. A gust of wind in the chimney sent out the plumes of sweet, blue smoke into the warm room. There was the intimate glow of a table lamp which focused its circle of light on my typewriter and picked up the white brightness of my pads of paper. On the walls, the strong primary colours of our prints glowed in the flickering firelight, the spines of the paperback books were a brilliant abstract impression in themselves. The thick rugs seemed to ripple with warmth in the cosy room. The cat rumbled contentedly. Upstairs, the baby was asleep.

I went to the kitchen and came back with a screwdriver. It would be easy to open the crate. The top panel with its rows of holes came away with three gentle probings of the screwdriver. I put the lid and its twisted staples on an armchair. Together, we looked down into the box, grimacing at the smell which sprang powerfully up from inside and eclipsed the sweetness of the fire, the scent of my wife's hair. There was a thick layer of straw; it moved a little with the sudden intrusion of light. I drew aside the bedding, moving gingerly and snatching away my hand. Ann chuckled and nudged my arm, but she would not reach down into the damp straw. The cat had withdrawn to a vantage point on top of the writing-desk, where it basked like a goddess in the circle of light. Its eyes were fixed on the crate, it sneezed quietly at the rising reek. Something was coming awake, shifting among the straw.

The crate creaked. A log spilled from its bed of coal and fell onto the hearth with a splintering of sparks. From out of its nest of straw, as though summoned by the signal from the fire, the bird put up its head. It yawned, showing a worm-like tongue and issuing a stink of seaweed.

Ann and I recoiled. The cat leapt onto the typewriter with an electric bristling of fur. Shedding its covering of straw, shaking itself free of its bedding, the bird rose out of the pit of its crate. The cormorant emerged in front of the fire. It lifted its wings clear of the box, hooked with its long beak onto the top of its wooden prison. Aroused from its slumbers by the direct heat of the flames, it heaved itself out of the box and collapsed on its breast on the carpet of the living-room. I felt Ann's hand at my arm, tugging me backwards. Together, we shrank to the foot of the stairs which led up from the room. The cat was quivering with surprise. And the cormorant picked itself up, straightened its ruffled feathers with a few deft movements of its beak, stretching out its tattered, black wings and shaking them, like an elderly clergyman flapping the dust from his gown. It sprang onto the sofa, where it raised its tail and shot out a jet of white-brown shit which struck the wooden crate with a slap before trickling towards the carpet.

Ann squealed and took three steps up.

'Get it out! For God's sake, get the thing outside!'

I stepped forward, instinctively reaching for a heavy cushion from an armchair, and advanced on the big, goose-like bird, wafting at its face with my weapon. The bird retreated. Its neck writhed and the horny beak made sporadic thrusts at the cushion. I forced it backwards into the corner by the writing-desk, as the cat fled with a loud hissing and its question-mark of a tail held up.

The cormorant went under the table, lodged itself among the legs and peered out, like an eel in its underwater lair. It shot a yellow jet into the skirting board, pattered its webbed feet wetly into the carpet.

'Get it into the crate! Get it out from under the table!'

Ann's voice was shrill with panic.

I reached for the box and turned it onto its side in the middle of the room, with the intention of driving the bird back into the prison. Straw fell out and steamed in the heat of the fire. By tapping bluntly on the table with the poker, I forced the cormorant out. By now, it had found its voice, an ugly, rasping yell which drew from the cat a series of spitting coughs. The bird leapt clumsily from its den, beat its wings just twice as it somersaulted through the air, knocking the lamp from its table and sending up a whirlwind of paper from around the typewriter. The lamp went out with a report like a pistol shot. The flames alone illuminated the little room, for Ann was too numb with horror to shift from her position of relative safety to reach the light switch. In the trembling glow of the fire, the bird awakened to a new frenzy. It threw itself about the room like a gigantic bat, croaking, squirting its shit, one moment hanging in the heavy curtains as though trapped with the moths and the craneflies, then achieving a series of laboured beats across the floor which ended in a panic-stricken collision with the pictures on one wall and the light shade which dangled from the centre of the ceiling. Books toppled from shelves as the cormorant thrust its beak into the crevices between them. I joined Ann on the stairs. Together we watched the hysteria of the cormorant, the bird which had been neatly delivered to us in its clean, white box. Even when it became calmer, the collapse of another log from the fire and its accompanying shower of sparks would set it mad again. It found the cat under the sofa and struck at it twice with its beak of black horn. For a second, it held tight on the cat's foreleg, catching it with breathtaking speed as the cat made its instinctive, raking defence, but the animal tugged free and was up the stairs, between our legs, as quick and as hot as one of the sparks from the fire. The bird worked out its anger and puzzlement in the living-room of our cottage while we could only watch, while the cat was hiding, wild-eyed, in the darkness of an upstairs cupboard, while the baby awoke and whined in confusion at the cries and the clattering impact of the struggle below, while another night of drizzling cloud descended on the mountains. The flames of the fire had their cosy, orange light shredded and shattered into a thousand splinters of red and green by the heavy, black wings of the cormorant. It spat out its gutteral shouts. It splashed the walls and the books with its gouts of shit. It made threatening forays to the stairs, where I cursed and lashed out with my slippered foot. It wondered at the glowing logs, retreated from a power it did not understand and could not intimidate.

Until, exhausted as much by its unmitigated bafflement as by its assault on the incomprehensible surroundings, it staggered suddenly and toppled into the upturned crate. The bird buried its head in the familiarly scented straw, heaving with tension and fatigue.

I stepped quickly from the shadows, righted the box and replaced the lid. The cormorant shuffled into the drying straw. Then it was quiet. Its panting breath sent up fumes of fish through the perforations. I sat carefully on the sofa, avoiding the stains. Ann was weeping softly on the stairs, the tears which collapsed into the corners of her mouth catching the golden lights of a dying fire.

The cormorant had been left to me and Ann in the will of my uncle. Uncle Ian was a bachelor, who had spent all his working life as a schoolteacher in Sussex. For him, the narrow confines of the country prep school and all the trivial politics of the staffroom were a prison from which he could joyously escape in the holidays on his wooden river-boat. He kept the boat on the tidal mudflats of the Ouse at Newhaven. It was afloat for only four hours at a time, but he could safely reach the county town of Lewes up the river, have a meal and a pint of the local bitter before swooping back towards the coast on the retreating tide. He made this voyage innumerable times, never tiring of the flat fields which stretched away on either side of the river, never wearying of the gulls and swans and herons which maintained their posts at the slow bends and reed beds. In the summer, the swallows and martins spun their dizzy aerial threads around the little boat. A sandpiper fled upstream and waited on the next flat of drying mud before whistling plaintively and fleeing once more from the intrusion of the rippling wash. At Piddinghoe, the sun caught the golden fish which is the weather vane of the village church and threw its reflection into the brown water. There were coot and moorhen among the reeds from which the heron raised its dignified head. In the autumn, Ian went upstream in the shrinking evenings and saw a tired sun extinguish itself behind the gentle barrier of the downs.

But it was on one of his rare winter journeys that he came across the cormorant. At first, in the failing light, he thought there was a clump of weed floating in midstream, and he had steered away to avoid catching it in his propeller. But, as he passed and saw that the dark mass in the water was a stricken bird, he turned and came in close. The cormorant, a first-year bird, was drowning. It had spread its wings in an attempt to remain afloat a little longer, but soon it was waterlogged, and the swirling tide simply turned it and stirred it, and the creeping cold was deep in the bones of the young bird. There was oil on its throat and in its face. When Ian lifted it carefully into the boat, he saw that the oil was in its wings, locking together the feathers. The cormorant was trying, with its failing strength, to preen the filthy oil from its breast: in doing so, it had swallowed it and gathered it in globules around its beak. The bird lay in the cabin of the boat and rested its black eyes on the boots of the man who had plucked it from the Ouse. It was a tough, young creature. It responded to Ian's ministrations, his cleaning and feeding. Where it had at first been passive, it grew demanding and rude, aiming its murder-beak at the hands of the old man who proffered fish and meat. By the spring, it was as arrogant and vicious and unpredictable, as preoccupied with the business of eating and shouting and shitting as any first-year cormorant. Ian doted on the bird. It seemed to him to have many of the characteristics of his colleagues in the staffroom and the pupils that he taught, yet without the hypocrisy which threw up a veneer of good manners.

The cormorant was a lout, a glutton, an ignorant tyrant. It affected nothing else.

Ian was told by his doctor that he would shortly die. This did not distress the elderly bachelor. His had been a lonely and a bitter life. He had found little in common with his company in school. Only the oily and rotten-smelling river and its everchanging skies had eased the disappointment of so many unfulfilling years. Something of the mischief of the cormorant had touched him as he went through the dreary business of making a will. He had a little cash to leave, the boat, a run-down cottage in the mountains of north Wales which he had ceased to visit and use once the long hours of travelling from Sussex began to be too much. And he had the cormorant. Strong as it was, it had become dependent on him for food. In a short time, through the spring and into the summer, he had seen that the bird would never learn to support itself. It had grown into an impressively ugly bird, a gangster of a creature, with its mantling black wings, the cocksure stance, the menacing angles of that horn-brown bill and its rubbery, webbed feet. It oozed the stink of fish, the smell of the river, it breathed the tang of the tides. But it had learned to feed from the hand of the man. The bubble-beaded pursuit of dabs in the waters of the Ouse was forgotten. He would leave it in his will to one of his relatives, distant as they were, and the bird would be supported and nourished like a child, like the children which Ian had never had.

And I was Ian's choice of beneficiary.

I hardly knew him. We had met over the years at weddings and funerals and the occasional family Christmas. Maybe he had been able to see something of himself in me, the germs of disillusionment in my boy's face. But, unlike Ian, I had married while Ann and I were students at a teacher-training college, and we had gone together into our jobs in a Midland school. We persevered in the face of uncooperative students, using unsuitable and often irrelevant textbooks, and we returned in the evenings to our suburban, semi-detached house. We met Ian at another funeral. Perhaps he could see, from the set of our eyes and the way of our voices, that Ann and I were not teachers, just as he had never really been a teacher. He liked me. And he told me

that Ann would make a good and loving wife. I remember my
hands were shaking from the cutting cold of the graveside. The
drizzle settled on my glasses and dripped like tears onto my
cheeks, into the sparse whiskers of my jaw. No, I was not a
teacher. And Ian must have thought that the gift of the cormorant
could rescue us from our routine Midland existence.

So he thought of me when he went to the office of his solicitor.
His will was quite simple. He left the few hundred pounds to
Harry, our baby son, and he left the cottage in Wales to me. He
knew that the building was sound, although it had been neglected
and had stood empty for several hard winters. It was only a tiny,
terraced cottage, with a couple of bedrooms, but it had a fair-sized
sitting-room with an open grate, a bathroom and a kitchen. There
was a garden which led down to a stream at the bottom. Being
snug in the middle of the terrace, it should have stayed dry
throughout the years of neglect. Perhaps the roof would need
some attention. He left the cottage to us, knowing from our
expressions at the bitter graveside the last time that we met,
that we would want to take it and make it a home with the money
from the sale of our property. And Ian made one binding condition:
the cottage should be ours for as long as we supported and
sustained the cormorant. The solicitor shrugged, but admitted
that the beneficiaries could be bound in such a way. The executor
of the will would monitor the progress and the welfare of the bird
and see that the conditions of the will were observed. It was
mischievous. But something of the cormorant's hooligan instincts
must have infected Ian in his final months and coloured his
philanthropy.

Uncle Ian died. He was on the boat one evening in June, moving
briskly with a rising tide from the wide waters of Piddinghoe
towards the rip under Southease bridge. He must have had pains
in his chest since leaving the moorings at Denton island, possibly
after a struggle to start the outboard motor. When he collapsed
onto the floor of the boat, he gripped at his seizing chest and
struck his head on the petrol tank. And, as he lay convulsing for
just a few seconds, the cormorant sat and watched. Only the
slow blinking of its eyes showed that any muscle stirred in its
green-black frame. The bird stared into the face of the dying man.

When the man lay still, his chest clenched in the rigour of death, when a dribble of saliva glistened on his chin, the cormorant dropped from its perch on the boat's cabin and landed with its wide, wet feet on his belly. The boat caught in the iron limbs of the bridge, held there by the tide and the busy thrusts of the propeller. A heron briefly raised its head from fishing and turned an eye of frost on the butting vessel. The cattle snorted and returned to the lush grass of the water meadows. That evening, another boat stopped alongside the little cruiser. They found the man, dead, on the floor. The cormorant flapped heavily away to avoid the threatening boots of the boarding party, but it followed the boats downriver to the rank and frothy waters of the moorings.

Ian was dead. And his cheeks were pitted from the blows of the cormorant's beak. His lips were torn. The tender tissues of his gums were split. One eye remained intact.

When they had taken the body away, the bird heaved itself onto the deck of its master's boat. It was seen through the rest of the evening and that warm summer's night, hunched on the top of the cabin. It only blinked and cleaned a few morsels of soft flesh from its beak.

This was the bird that we inherited.

We had been in the cottage for a week when the cormorant was delivered, that October evening. We had leapt at the opportunity of leaving our work in the Midlands. The sale of our house there gave us the financial freedom to have the cottage quickly surveyed and a few repairs carried out. Basically it was sound. A builder replaced a number of slates on the roof and some of the wiring was seen to. Soon, with our books and prints and brightly coloured rugs, the little place was cosy and warm. The village nestled under the cloud-covered summit of Snowdon, on the road between Caernarfon and Beddgelert. There was a shop, a post office and a pub. I stocked up with logs and coal; the fire gilded our living-room with its scented flames and sent up a tall feather of smoke into the autumn air. I was content to stay at home throughout the day and devote my time to the writing of my history text-book, exasperated as I had been in my experience as a teacher by the unsuitability of the material. Furthermore, I could manage Harry, our boy of eleven months, in the intervals of my work. Ann straight away found work in the pub, helping with the preparation of bar snacks at lunchtime and in the evenings until about nine o'clock. People in the village were friendly, but wary at first. We knew it would take time to make real friends there, by the nature of the mountains and the wet plantations. Being English was not a disadvantage, contrary to our expectations. The pub, the shop and the post office were all in the hands of English couples who had fled the northern cities of England to find a cleaner and less frantic way of life in the Welsh hills. There was no novelty in our being English; we were simply another young family who had come to settle in the village.

The news of the death of Uncle Ian was a surprise to us. But our inheritance of the cottage seemed to be a miracle, such a thunderbolt of good fortune that the matter of the cormorant was practically ignored as an eccentric novelty perpetrated by my uncle, as a joke. We set our minds on quitting school and beginning a new life in Wales. I had a notion of what the bird would be like: it would be gawky and angular, a sort of black sea-goose, I gathered from a handbook, with an extraordinarily healthy appetite for fish. Well, it could stay in the backyard, on the end of a leash perhaps, or potter around and scavenge like a farmyard goose. We bought fish for the cat anyway, so it would be no trouble to double the ration and feed the cormorant at the same time. It was a sure sign of our complacency in receipt of the cormorant that we had opened the white wooden crate in our living-room and expected some kind of placid, domestic fowl to emerge and be driven quietly out through the back door. The image of the sea-raven, hunched and black and indelibly marked with the stink of mud and fish, the slow-blinking cormorant which had set its beak to the cheeks and gums of its saviour . . . this had been forgotten in the euphoria of moving into our rural retreat. The turmoil of the bird's first appearance by the flaming lights of the fire had upset our picture of domestic bliss. It came from its box as ugly and as poisonous as a vampire bat.

During a night of tears and recriminations, a long, sleepless night when the name of Uncle Ian came in for repeated vilification, we began to face up to that seemingly innocuous clause in the will which stipulated that the cormorant would be a part of our life in the cottage, or else the cottage would be forfeited. The next morning, before the baby could be brought downstairs, I manhandled the crate out of the living-room and put it down carefully in the yard. For all the sound and movement which was evident from within, the bird could have been dead. But that was wishful thinking on my part. In any case, there was some ludicrous clause which forbade us from disposing of our charge by releasing it or killing it; its death on the first day of our responsibility would have looked somewhat suspicious if we were to attempt to construe it as an accident. Undoubtedly, the bird was alive in the fetid straw of the box. Its smells simmered through the panel of perforations.

Ann came down the stairs, still smudging the tears of disbelief from her face. She set about the living-room with water and disinfectant. While she washed the paintwork and sponged vigorously at the curtains, the furniture, the pictures, the books and our precious rugs, I was busy in the yard with my hammer and nails. I hastily erected a sort of cage in one corner, a ramshackle structure of chicken-wire and woodwork, with a section of corrugated iron on the top to afford some weather protection. Into this, I tipped the cormorant. I pushed in the crate, having loosened the lid again, knocked it over with a wary foot and shook out the contents into the new cage. There was a bundle of damp straw, that was all. Nothing stirred. I had seen the same sort of thing in zoos: rows of big cages, each with its informative little sign, and nothing but a bank of straw at the back, in which, if the signs were to be believed, some exotic and possibly savage beast was snoozing. But not a flicker of life. So, after I had closed down the walls of chicken-wire with a series of nails, I took a cane from the shed and tentatively pushed it into the cage and into the mess of straw. One moment the straw lay silent and still. Then it exploded in a chaos of black wings and spitting cries. The cormorant erupted from sleep, flung itself at the wire. Its jabbing bill came through, it hung for a second, scrabbling with its fleshy feet, its wings outstretched on the wire, like some gas-crazed soldier on a

French battlefield. I yelped and jumped back. I watched in horror as the bird fell to the ground and began to strut backwards and forwards across the floor of its confines, until it became calmer. It pecked a little at the ground, threw some of the straw in the air and found some nameless morsel hidden among it. I watched the workings of the bird's throat. Something slid down into the mucous darkness. At least the cormorant was behind bars.

Ann came into the yard and looked at the bird from the back door. She was holding Harry in her arms. He was agog at the spectacle of the cormorant, throwing out his arms and wriggling like a trout. The bird froze for a moment, slowly opened up its wings into a black shroud and croaked. It came to the wire. Snaking its neck, it hissed a long, malodorous hiss and brought up a pellet of half-digested matter which lay steaming in the weak sunshine. Harry gaped at the offering and tried to get free from Ann. Something told her that this was not suitable viewing for her baby boy. Without speaking, she turned back into the kitchen, with Harry swivelling his little blond head for a last glimpse of the cormorant.

I opened a tin of cat food and managed to shove it under the wire, on a tin plate. The bird devoured the meat before standing on the plate and releasing one long jet of yellow shit where the food had been a minute before. I found myself fascinated by the cormorant's manners. I knew of football supporters and pop stars whose behaviour in railway carriages and expensive hotels was lovingly reported in the lightweight press and who were alleged to be like this, wonderfully oblivious to accepted standards of decency and cleanliness. But this bird made an art of being vile. It was somehow endearing, such candour. I turned away from the kitchen window, in case Ann should see my expression and disapprove of my smiles. Uncle Ian must have felt the same about the bird. I fed it again and supplied it with fresh water, forgot about my writing for the rest of the day as I strengthened the cage and effected a sort of hatch which would make feeding easier. I stayed close to the cormorant in the backyard, going into the cottage to look after the baby while Ann was out, but returning to watch the bird. It waddled around the cage, panting. When it had drunk deeply from the bowl, it put its face down into the water and snorted through its fur-covered nostrils. The bird held up its wings and flapped them until a few black feathers dropped onto the slate floor. By the afternoon, the cage was spattered with droppings, to which the sprinklings of down and dust and straw had stuck and through which the bird went slapping with its wide feet. I saw that frequent hosing would have to constitute part of the new routine initiated by the arrival of the cormorant. But if I could establish some kind of relationship, simply by being the regular supplier of food and water, perhaps the new member of the family would not cause too severe a disruption of our lives. I watched the bird for the first afternoon and allowed it to watch me. Maybe it could become a manageable entity. Harry must be kept away from it, and then its unpredictable temper and lack of hygiene would not be a hazard.

The bird: it would be about eighteen months old, if Uncle Ian had rescued it from the river in its first winter. By now, it was three feet long from the tip of its tail feathers to the end of its beak. It was by no means utterly black when looked at in the sunlight and when it was behaving calmly, although I had thought of it as uniformly coal-black in the midst of its lunatic fits in the living-room, on the previous evening. In fact, it was shot through with browns and greens and blues as the sun caught it on its back and wings, the iridescence of oil and the stale river. There was a lighter patch on its breast, which the handbook said was the mark of an immature bird: this would disappear and the cormorant would become completely sooty. Its beak was an impressive weapon of heavy horn, three inches in length, brown and smooth, hooked at the tip. The bird stalked around on its webbed feet, putting them down with a slap in the water and in its own many-coloured squirts of shit. It held itself upright, like a goose, hissed with its bill open and made a nasal croaking. The cormorant was a Heathcliff, a Rasputin, a Dracula. Or maybe it was just a sea-crow, *corvus marinus*, as the name suggested, just a scavenging, unprincipled crow. The name came to me in a flash: Archie. I would call the cormorant Archie. It was harsh, like the sound the bird repeatedly croaked. There was something cocky and irreverent about it.

And in the evening, when twenty-four hours had elapsed since the opening of the crate, our mountain cottage seemed to have recaptured the peace and cosiness which the arrival of the bird had destroyed. Ann came in from work. It was raining again. She was breathless and a little flushed from her short bicycle ride, there were jewels of fine drizzle in her hair and on her eyelashes. When she smiled, I saw the pale blue opacity of her teeth, I kissed her and tasted her clean, metallic tongue. She went upstairs to take off her coat and to see that Harry was asleep. In the living-room, the fire was banked up with coal and a white, bitter-smelling log of horse chestnut. Everything was clean and warm. The cat lay curled on a cushion, its head lost in the thick fur of its body, its sleep a safe oblivion. I had been working on the textbook, with the pool of light thrown onto my typewriter by the table lamp. All was at peace. Ann came down, having brushed her hair until it burned in many different reds and browns, the colours of the autumn which the night outside had hidden. We sat on the rug, close to the flames of the fire, and again we kissed. The fire spat. There was a flurry of wet wind on the window. Together, we gently collapsed and lay in the soft cocoon of our cottage. And soon, when the fire was low and the lights it had shone so brightly had begun to fade into ochre, when the embers sighed and tumbled inwards to be swallowed in their own secret furnace, we went upstairs to bed.

We awoke to the screaming of gulls.

It was just light. Ann shoved me and sat up in bed, instantly alert to the cries of the baby. She heard Harry, but his weak noises were blurred in the frantic chorus outside our bedroom window. In a moment, she had gone to his room and picked him out of his cot, returning with him to the warmth of the double bed. I reached over, rubbing my eyes, and pulled open the curtains.

The backyard was a snowstorm of gulls. They wheeled in a maelstrom of white and grey and black. Their cries broke in the cold morning air, a hundred voices of the sea and the blowing spray, focused on the small expanse of garden. The gulls dropped into the yard, rose again on the strength and elasticity of their wings. They came close to the window, the herring gulls circling with throats distended to issue their bullying laughter. The black-headed gulls threw out their bilious cries. And among the gulls' cacophony, there came the repeated croaks of the cormorant, as though it had summoned the gulls and was ordering their riotous congregation. We watched from the window. Harry chuckled and thrust his hands forward. His cheeks became flushed, he shouted something in a rasping tone. I put on some trousers and an old pullover, stepped into my slippers and went downstairs. Through the kitchen window I saw the gulls swirling like a blizzard around the cage, then up to our bedroom, their wings beating against the glass. I heard Ann's shriek, heard her tug the curtain closed again. I heard Harry's ugly shouts.

The cormorant stood with its chest pressed against the wire, its neck extended and the murder-beak jutting through. It had outstretched its wings and hooked them somehow onto the wire, gripping there like some prehistoric bird with clawed fingers. Archie stood erect, croaking and hissing, a black, malignant priest in a multitude of angels. I put on a coat, quickly found some cat food. There was an old, threadbare blanket in the airing cupboard, which I took out and threw over my arm. Then I stepped into the yard.

First of all, the gulls recoiled from the garden, evaporated up and over the surrounding trees. Archie was silent. Still the cormorant hung on the wire. But, with a series of hoarse cries from that horny beak, the gulls returned and dived around my head with a crescendo of screams. They rained their soapy droppings on the slates and on my shoulders. The birds came down until I felt the buffeting of their wings. The air was filled with the smell of brine and fish. I lurched forward, shoving the plate of food into the cage. The cormorant turned, tore itself from the wire, leaving behind a few black feathers. It came for my hands. But I withdrew as the beak came close. I put the blanket over the front of the cage and secured it with a number of slates. Archie was silent again, distracted by the meat, and soon the gulls dispersed. The cormorant was gone. There was no longer anything in the backyard to summon their hysterical presence.

This was Archie.

Ann shuddered at the sight of the cormorant, its demonic arrogance. She held Harry to her breast and twisted his face towards her own. But the child flung a sidelong glance in the direction of the cage, beating the air with his fist. Brilliantly flushed, his eyes glittering with ice, he was suffused with the malice of the sea-crow.

TWO

In the fortnight which followed, I began to find that I could exercise more control over Archie. The bird became accustomed to the man who came each morning with food, and it no longer made its snaking thrusts at my hands. Instead, it watched from the far corner of its cage while I opened the hatch and eased the iron plate through the wire, before it walked like a duchess towards the meat. Archie ate with a flurry of bolting gulps, taking a beakful and then stretching up its head to ease the food into the gullet. I saw the meat slipping downwards, a bulge in the throat, working and moving like a live thing. Every afternoon, it was time to hose out the cage with a fine spray of water. All the accumulated droppings sped across the slates in foaming milk, pieces of straw and discarded fish, the walnut-sized pellets of indigestible matter, it all washed out of the cage and into the nettle beds of the little garden. Archie spread its wings and held its face up to the flying water. It stood under the shower with its beak open, allowing the water to course over its tongue and its half-closed eyes, down its oily breast. The cormorant shook off the water with a vigorous beating of its wings. It shivered from top to toe, like a wet dog, and the droplets flew across the backyard in a confetti of blues and greens and silver.

But the bird could not stay inside its cage for ever. Sooner or later, it would be time to bring it out and let it have some exercise. Now that it was used to its new breadwinner, I began to foresee the time when Archie would even go free, as it had begun to do for Uncle Ian, and still return for its food. First of all, it would suffice to bring Archie out on a leash. One crisp November afternoon, while Ann was at work and Harry was sound asleep upstairs, I decided to attempt to exercise the bird. I gave it a

small dish of cat food, only a couple of beakfuls, to distract it long
enough for me to secure it on a length of rope. As the cormorant
bent to the meat, I approached. I had put on my wellington boots
and a pair of gardening gloves as protection against the beak. The
meal was placed near the hatch, to bring the bird within range.
It was disconcertingly easy: Archie obligingly placed one foot into
the noose which I had put onto the floor in front of the plate, and,
from the safety afforded by the barrier of chicken-wire, the rope
was gently pulled tighter until the knot was snug around the bird's
ankle. Archie hardly glanced up from the plate. It continued to
swallow each morsel with familiar speed, as though at any moment
the remaining food would be confiscated. I waited for it to finish.
At the final gulp, Archie turned towards me, stared and blinked,
yawned a long, creaking yawn, a gentle kiss of fish breath. I
opened the hatch.

   Archie waddled out into the yard. It was a cold, clean afternoon,
lit by a watery sun. The sky was blue and empty of gulls. I left
the rope slack, and the bird stalked into the garden, pushing its
head among the long grass. It glanced up at the sky and shook
out its wings, but it folded them again carefully, pushing away a
few feathers with the preening of its beak. I allowed Archie to
lead me further from the cage, towards the stream which ran
past the foot of the garden. At the sight of the water, the
cormorant increased its pace. There it stood on a slippery boulder
and watched the tumbling brook. In a calmer pool, it trod boldly
down and floated like a duck, paddling its feet to maintain position
in the current. It put its head under the water and tugged at the
weed. The stream brought along a clustered spawn of bubbles,
leaves from the oak and ash which lined the water, twigs and
acorns which the bird inspected and sieved with its inquisitive
bill. Archie floated low in the current, the water ran across its
back like mercury. The bird relaxed and filled itself with the
half-remembered rhythm of tides.

   I sat down on a dry boulder a little way upstream and wound
the rope a few times around my wrist, allowing a little slack so
that Archie could move about the slower pool and venture into
the swifter currents.

   I thought about Uncle Ian: a grey, anonymous man, embedded

in a grey, anonymous school, a man whose features I had never really noticed. We had met so seldom, usually at a graveside, with our carefully polished shoes side by side in the soil, hearing the customary graveside words and the drumming of earth on a coffin of new wood. I knew little about him. He had been a teacher, but his heart was never in it; he was irritable with his boys and curt with the other members of staff. He had never married. He must have spent the long evenings after school in his musty flat, just a hundred yards from the Channel coast, where the spray spattered the window frames until orange tears of rust stained the building, where the salt gathered like frost on the panes of glass. In the holidays, he rubbed and painted the boat on the mudflats behind Denton island. When the rain came or it was too cold to work, he would sit alone inside the cabin, with his cigars and a bottle of beer. The swans came and demanded feeding, soaking the crusts of a sandwich in the water of a tidal pool before drawing them down and down the emaciated columns of their necks. He might flick them the butt of a cigar and watch them recoil, nauseated. It was Ian's little joke. And in his final year, he had the cormorant to occupy him over a bitter Sussex winter. Whatever love he had stored up and barely touched in the recesses of his soul, he must have spent on the bird. He restored it to rude health. Somewhere within Uncle Ian, under the greyness of his disappointments, behind his gruff and apparently wilful gracelessness, there must have been a reservoir of love, as good as new, never sullied by the pitfalls of human companionship. The one time he had reached into this untapped fund, the cormorant had answered with such passionate kisses as tore away the flesh of his cheeks, his lips, his gums. The fresh soil had rained also on the wood of Ian's coffin. I was at the graveside, with my shoes in mud. The rain trickled into the sparse hairs of my beard and poppled my glasses. My hands shook with the cold until I felt for the warmth of Ann's fingers. Uncle Ian had thought of us in his last few months. Archie had come from Sussex to the mountains of Wales, like an orphan, lost and hurt in the company of strangers. It was a strange gift. Ours was a bizarre duty.

The roar of a low-flying jet broke the peace of the autumn

afternoon. At the buffeting noise, the cormorant sprang from the water as though an electric charge had been passed through it, landing on the grassy bank of the stream in a disarray of wet feathers. For a moment, Archie scrabbled to get a foothold and lay on its breast, unable to find a purchase with its unsuitable feet. The jet howled on its way and left behind a thunder of bruised air. The bird stood up. It blinked and came at me like a farmyard gander, the head held low, the beak agape, hissing. For Archie, the breach of its calm in the cold pool must be attributed to the presence of a man: the noise was a man-noise and the man was a threat. I jumped to my feet and retreated before the determined bird, cracking the length of rope and sending a loop like a wave along it, which finally snapped against the cormorant's belly. This, and the size of the green wellingtons, was too much for Archie; backing off, it began to shake itself. A shower of icy water flew from its slick black plumage. I tugged the bird towards the wire cage. Again, it was a simple task to lure Archie into captivity with the replenished plate of cat food. Leaving the line attached to the bird's ankle for future use, tying it through the mesh onto the kitchen drainpipe, I securely closed the hatch. Archie was back in the cage and no damage was done. I looked forward to telling Ann when she came in from work.

It became increasingly easier to take Archie into the garden and down to the stream for his afternoon exercise. I enjoyed the hours I spent with the cormorant, and the bird began to treat me as though I were an acceptable part of its environment. I sat with my boots in the water and felt the teeth of the cold gnawing on my toes, through my feet and into my ankles. It was a marvel that Archie was content to float there, half submerged, to explore the depths of its pool without being affected by the temperature. At night, the bird returned to the white wooden crate in which it had been delivered, snuggling down into the pit of straw. There was once a visit from the executor of the will, one of my cousins. He was a suave young executive, disappointed not to have benefited under the will; it was quite clear that he would have been glad to find either that the cormorant was being neglected by the fortunate couple who had inherited the cottage or that the bird was proving to be a really intolerable addition to our family.

In fact, he saw that Archie was thriving, growing into a sleek and haughty creature. Our routine had comfortably accommodated the bird. We did not mention the uproar caused by Archie's first emergence from the box, nor the congregation of gulls. I smiled behind my hands to see the cormorant on its best behaviour: it lunged like a wild cat at the man in the city suit when he put out a hand to inspect the cage; it hung on the wire in a spasm of rage. As a peace offering to the astonished visitor, a steaming pellet was delivered after a second's laboured retching, and a squirt of shit nearly reached the city shoes. Archie was on top form. I winked at Ann, who was watching from the kitchen window, but she turned away, rolling her eyes at the ceiling.

The weeks passed. Autumn in the mountains, with its scent of pine resin and the damp decay of oak leaves, changed to winter. The air clenched its fists. There was a period of dry, crackling cold. Morning was a silent world of frost, when each clump of bracken was as brittle as glass, as sharp as a razor. In the afternoon, the sky turned darker quickly, discolouring like an old bruise. The cormorant waited in the corners of its cage, waited as though its bones would crack under the strain of the creaking frost. I piled up the straw and the bird sought refuge in it. I was tempted to stay inside and play with Harry, who was beginning to walk a few tottering steps. Ann came in each evening, and her kisses were the kisses of ice: her cheeks, her nose and even her metallic tongue were beaded with ice. We heaped up the grate with more coal and more logs as the night outside squeezed the cottage. Before it was bedtime, the little boy was encouraged to walk up and down the length of the hearth rug, collapsing at the end of each successful journey into the arms of his mother. But his concentration was sometimes broken by the crackling of the logs. He whirled round at the explosion of sparks and put up a hand to the smoke which was blown back down the chimney. Then he would sit down heavily, bemused by the fire. I had to lift him away from it, as his fingers went out in the direction of the flames. There was something more than a child's ordinary attraction to the fire: Harry's face became clouded over, he was lost to us for a second or two.

The time came to take the bird out with me on my searches

for firewood. I set up a partition in the back of the van, as the owners of dogs have for their pets, and drew the cormorant along on its leash before urging it, with a threatening movement of the boot, to hop up into the vehicle. Again, it was wonderful how easy it was to manoeuvre Archie with the help of a plateful of cat food as the persuasive factor; apparently, it would sublimate any other desire to the call of its appetite. With the bird ensconced in the back, I drove down the Caernarfon road towards the coast. There were looks of dismay from the drivers of following cars as Archie flattened itself against the rear window, wings outspread, the mighty sea-crow raging against captivity. Stopping near the castle, I opened up the car and tugged out the cormorant, which collapsed at first on its chest in the puddles of the harbour car park. I led the bird firmly across the swing bridge, keeping it close to my green boots and shouting in advance to warn away curious pedestrians. Children, especially, evinced an extraordinary desire to offer themselves as targets for Archie's beak: there was something in the whiteness of their hands and the chubby legs of toddlers which brought a glint to the cormorant's eye. By the time we reached the beach, we had attracted a small but enthusiastic following. But there, among the seaweed and the rock pools, with the authentic smell of the sea, the salt in every sniff of the air, Archie was oblivious to its admirers. The bird went to the end of the rope and stretched itself until the sinews sang. It opened up the wings like the remains of an ancient gamp, buffeted the breeze from the Menai Straits. Archie croaked. It sent up a flock of oyster-catchers in a whirling cloud of black and white. The cormorant croaked again and conjured a fragile mist of dunlin. The old heron beat away towards the flatter beaches of Anglesey, a pair of crows set off to their place on the walls of the castle. Untangling the entire length of rope, I attached the other end to the weathered wood of the groyne. The cormorant was afloat in a matter of seconds, moving from the beach like a semi-submerged submarine, dark and sleek. I gathered armfuls of driftwood. Archie dived and surfaced with dabs from the sandy floors of the straits, its hunting instinct revived. The aching cold crept into another November afternoon, twilight fell over the shoulders of the castle and settled on the black water. Lights sprang up like fireflies all over the old town. I took the wood back to the car and returned for Archie. It was easy to draw the bird into the shore and over the seaweed-slippery rocks of the beach. Archie was tired. It lay in the back of the van, burrowed into the straw, barely moving as I drove from Caernarfon into the mountains of Snowdon. Full of dabs and sea air, the cormorant tumbled into its wooden crate, disappeared among the warm bedding. The driftwood was laid to dry in a basket in front of the hearth, breathing out the fumes of seaweed.

Many times, we spent the hours of the winter afternoons among the boulders of the beach. The cormorant learned to follow me, in pursuit of the green wellingtons. The rope remained around Archie's ankle, but it seemed, on those evenings when the scent of wood fires from seaside cottages mingled with the sweat of the falling tide, that the bird knew the value of staying close, as it had stayed close to Uncle Ian even as a dead man.

There was firewood to be found, too, in the sheds of the mouldering old slate quarries of Nantlle. Here the bird could indulge another of its predatory instincts. I took Archie up to the mines one dismal day at the end of November. When the cormorant baulked at the bottom of the slate steps which climbed to the abandoned workings, I bent without thinking and picked it up under one arm. It was strange, I thought, I had never touched the bird before, always avoiding contact, always manoeuvring it with tugs of the rope or gestures of the boot. This time, Archie submitted to me and sat still in the crook of my arm as I walked up and up the grey slabs which wound between heaps of discarded shards. In a few minutes, we were a hundred feet above the village. From this vantage point, I could see up the valley towards the summit of Snowdon, smothered in its own private blanket of drizzle. On the lake, a flock of gulls was sprinkled like the ash of a forgotten cigarette. To the north, the sea spangled under a patch of sunlight. I put Archie on the ground again and led it over the miners' track to the empty buildings of the quarry. The place had been deserted by its community for thirty years. It was peopled by the gentle ghosts of the village. In the sheds and the offices were the ordinary relics of the miners: a rusty kettle in a back kitchen; the china cups and saucers of innumerable tea-breaks; the skeleton of a typewriter, with a sheet of yellowing paper in place, as though its owner had been called away from beginning his letter; pencils and rotten elastic bands in the offices; abandoned tools in the warehouses, some with the initials of the owners marked in the wooden handles; the manager's telephone on his desk, black and ugly as a charred bone. The rain through the roof had rotted the floor-boards. Jackdaws had stubbornly dropped their twigs into the chimneys, persisting in their folly until the debris filled up the grates and overflowed onto the planks. I tiptoed through the empty rooms. Plaster blew from the walls, as fine as flour. Somewhere a door was banging in the wind, hammering its irregular beat, the ghost of an obsolete miner. A rat fled along the corridor.

And it was the rats which sent a shudder of excitement through the cormorant. Archie bristled like a tom cat, clattered to the end of the rope. The bird flapped its wings and croaked the sea-crow threats. So I tied the leash to a window-frame in order to allow Archie plenty of scope for hunting, while I set to work collecting firewood, the splinters of abandoned pallets, old boards which I could split with my hatchet. In the next room, I could hear the patter of the cormorant's feet on the floor, its manic cries. I went to the door to watch. It was only a game, it seemed, for the rat which emerged from the skirting was big and brave. Archie had no intention of closing with it. The rat stood on its hind legs, like a pocket grizzly bear, swayed and snickered. The cormorant beat the air with its wings, sending up a cloud of dust. The rat and the cormorant continued their threatening displays until honour was satisfied, and the rat slid back into the darkness. Archie rearranged a few dishevelled feathers. But the bird was curious, it trembled with the thrill of the confrontation and went from room to room as far as the rope would allow, hissing at the holes in the skirting boards. The rats were a challenge. They made the dabs seem tame.

In spite of my growing confidence with Archie, Ann maintained a wary distance. She wanted nothing to do with the bird, leaving its cleaning and feeding and exercise entirely in my hands. Harry could now walk steadily around the house and showed a lively curiosity in any ornaments, books, pots and pans which his stubby fingers could reach. Ann was forever impressing on me the importance of keeping the boy away from the cormorant. Just because it consented to being stroked and even occasionally being picked up by its guardian did not mean that it would respect the tender little toddler. I knew this, I had seen Archie accelerate to the end of its leash in pursuit of small children on the beach at Caernarfon. Whenever the boy went into the garden, I had to manhandle him, struggling, away from the cormorant's cage. Harry would learn, we hoped, to count the big black bird among the hazards of his baffling new world, but for the time being he headed straight towards the cage at the slightest opportunity. And at such moments, the child's face became clouded over, his features seemed blurred in the overwhelming desire to reach out for the cormorant. Harry's chuckles were ugly as I swung him back into the kitchen, chuckles which were answered by the rasping cries of Archie.

Ann invited a number of her new friends from the village to see the cottage and the baby. Whenever I had the chance, sometimes to Ann's obvious irritation, I would proudly mention our unusual pet, and in the backyard our visitors might manage an outburst of appalled laughter at the sight of Archie. So that was the cormorant, a bird like a caricature of goose and crow, the likes of which Ann's friends had never ever seen, even on the screens of their televisions. It was mischievous, I knew, but I told Ann that the creature was a permanent feature of our life in the village and it did no harm to show it to the neighbours. I did not meet people so easily. I was either bent over the typewriter, feeding Harry in Ann's absence, or out in the van with Archie. To the neighbours, I must have seemed rather an outlandish figure. They heard the clacking of the typewriter even through the thick walls of the terrace. Over the garden fence, I would be seen with the hose, directing the spray onto the droppings which spattered the slates. They would hear me sometimes talking to the bird, swearing loudly at the tangle of rope, they saw me emerge from the cottage with my ragged pet and lift it by the neck into the back of the van. Children and cats were warned not to stray into the Englishman's garden. Only the gulls dropped down and cried into the face of the creature in its cage. I realised how odd all this must seem and smiled at the apparent eccentricity. I knew that I was only an escaping schoolteacher who had run from the routine of the suburban Midlands to bash out another ordinary textbook. But meanwhile I would enjoy my role as the man with the cormorant. Archie watched me with an enigmatic eye.

In the afternoons, when Ann's visitors were her young friends from the pub kitchen, who would come for endless cups of tea and the comparison of different brands of baby foods, I excused myself and went out with the bird. There was ratting to be done in the quarry offices, firewood to be gleaned from the seashore. The women raised their eyebrows and shrank to the corners of the room as I came through from the yard with Archie under my arm. The cormorant obliged with a snaking of its neck, the issue of fish breath. Usually I could make it through the front door before Archie lifted the stiff feathers of its tail and shot the shit onto the pavement. The women squealed and put their hands to their faces. And then, at last, we could drive away in the peace of the little humming van, into the plantations for easy pickings of pine splinters, or towards the coast. Now Archie could be trusted to sit in the passenger seat beside me. The bird peered through the windscreen. It thrust its head into the slipstream and sucked in the rushing cold air. I always slowed down drastically when we were passing a cyclist, to give him or her the full benefit of seeing the jabbing face of the cormorant at close quarters. There was once the pleasure of unseating an elderly gentleman, who bellowed in horror before toppling from his bicycle into a bed of nettles. Archie and I laughed all the way to Caernarfon. Horses and dogs were also fair game. Archie beat its wings at the window, the great sea-crow on the way to its hunting ground. Any other beasts, on four legs or two, were best to quail before the cormorant. Only I could approach Archie without its frenzied threats.

The weather softened as December arrived. There was talk of Christmas on the radio, and decorations in the pub. I returned from one outing with the bird, with a shapely little fir tree surreptitiously dug from the plantation. In the evening, at nine o'clock, Ann came home. I had had a good session at the writing, Harry was bathed and fed and ready for bed. There was a lovely fire and a number of logs warming on the hearth, waiting their turn to fuel the flames. Everything was in order. Ann awarded me a congratulatory kiss for my efforts. The cat leapt up from its buzzing sleep and scrabbled its claws on the side of an armchair. so I sent it through to the kitchen. And while the child sat starry-eyed on the sofa, agog at the brilliance of light and colour, we decorated the tree. There were mugs of soup, I lit a cigar, the tree became a fairy-tale tree and the room glowed. When it was done, the boy slipped from the couch and went unsteadily to the tree. While we watched, breathless and silent, Harry stood and reached out a hand to touch the fresh green needles. He put his face to them, sniffing like a dog. Then he turned, with a smile of ecstasy on his face, a glistening bubble at his mouth and his eyes lit with excitement. It was his Christmas tree, he knew it. Ann felt for my fingers and squeezed them hard. A scratching at the door reminded us that only the cat was missing the festivity, evicted from its customary territory in front of the fire. The smile on Harry's face froze for a split-second, worked itself into a lop-sided grin. With a hoarse cry, he staggered towards the door.

He strained on tiptoe to reach the handle, could not quite stretch his fingers high enough, howled over his shoulder for one of us to help.

'Calm down, Harry,' Ann said, as she got up from the sofa. 'It's hardly an emergency. Mummy's coming . . .'

The scratching continued. Cursing the cat's claws and the inevitably marked paintwork, she went to the door. Harry reached up again, failed to touch the knob. I could not tell whether he was weeping or laughing, there was only a series of blurred shouts. Ann swept him up and dumped him back on the sofa. She opened the door, squealed and stepped backwards.

The cat came into the room, tottering like a drunk. It lurched into the side of an armchair, rolled on its side with claws flailing at the fabric. With another desperate effort, as Ann recoiled and

I stood up in dismay, the cat collapsed on the hearth rug. Its face was a mask of blood. With every rasping breath, bubbles of mucous blood blew from the mess where the mouth had been. There were no eyes, only a cowl of scarlet, glistening wet in the firelight. Blood simmered deep in the throat. Only the blubbering movement in the middle of the mask betrayed the existence of the cat's nostrils, there was only blood in a gout where the cat's face had been. The animal fell on the rug. A long sigh came from the throat, it relaxed suddenly until a series of spurts of urine flowed, strong at first then falling to a trickle over the belly. The cat lay still. But a whisper broke from its chest, its body shuddered. The cat lay still.

The room was silent.

Until a log split open with a snap among the flames of the fire. And Harry's chuckles rang out. His face was brilliant with exhilaration, ablaze with pleasure. He beat his little hands together.

Ann sprang forward and picked him up. She hurried upstairs with him, her cheeks wet with tears. Harry swivelled his head wildly as he disappeared from the room.

I swore at length, before I picked up the cat on the coal shovel and moved through into the kitchen. The back door was ajar, the cat had just come in from the yard. The kitchen light lit up the yard and the garden. I left the shovel by the door and went outside. The hatch on the side of Archie's cage was flapping loose. The cage was empty. The cormorant's leash trailed down the garden towards the stream. I took up the rope but I did not pull. Running it through my hands, I followed it away from the lights of the cottage, until a resistance was felt in a jerking movement, like the fighting of a fish on an angler's line. This time, I began to tug, tugging at first, then sending the rest of the rope in a whiplash curve, disappearing in the gloom.

Archie came out of the shadows.

The cormorant was all black. It stood up straight and faced me. In the darkness, Archie was all black, its wings held out in a mockery of benediction. The bird came at me in two leaps, brandishing the heavy beak, punishing the night shadows with the power of its wing beats. There was blood on its bill. The broad

feet shone red. Among the ruffled feathers of its breast were
smears of sappy gore where it had begun to clean its face. I
kicked out with my slippered foot and the bird flapped backwards,
long enough for me to take up some slack around my wrist and
reel it in, retreating to the lights of the kitchen. Archie resisted,
skidded forward on slippery feet. As I fumbled with the hatch,
the cormorant struck hard at my hand. Swearing, lashing out, I
caught the bird's throat, lifted it up sharply and held it away from
me at arm's length. The feathers flew about my head, the winter
night stormed around me in the narrow confines of the backyard,
I opened the hatch wide and flung the cormorant inside like a
bundle of rags. My hand was bleeding. I secured the cage with
more than my accustomed thoroughness and went back into the
cottage.

Slipping the dead cat into the dustbin, I covered it with cold
ashes from the previous day's fire. There was nobody in the
living-room. I could hear Ann's low, musical voice in the bedroom
above my head, the answering chuckles of the boy. Before she
could come downstairs, I went to work on the stains of blood and
urine which the cat, in its death throes, had left on the hearth-rug.
Still wet, they shifted easily with vigorous rubbing. The scents
of soup, sizzling wood and the needles of pine were gone,
obliterated by the ammoniac whiff of disinfectant. The room
seemed shabby: the fire was fading, there were brown-ringed
bowls and spoons left lying on the carpet, my cigar had gone out,
stale and neglected. There was no warm woman or child, no cat.
I put some coal on the fire and chucked the butt of my cigar into
the grate. When Ann came down, she was a different woman.
She was stone, she was ice. She shed no tears for the cat, her
cat which she had taken in years before, before she had met me.
Ann was drained from her performance with Harry, disguising
her nausea for the sake of the child. Unable to speak, she sat in
silence and stared at the fire.

'It was Archie, it got out of the cage,' I said.

She turned her face to me blankly, as though I had addressed
her in a foreign language.

'Your hand . . .'

I had forgotten my hand as I cleaned up the room. Blood ran

down my fingers into the edges of my nails, but it was drying, a blackening crust.

'It got me when I was trying to stick it back in the cage. I'd better wash it . . .'

'Come on,' she said. 'I'll do it,' and she stood up, drawing me with her into the kitchen. I let her put my hand under the tap and clean it with soap. There were two ragged cuts half an inch long which she dabbed with a stinging disinfectant. She ignored my wincing, she was looking through the window into the area of light, watching the cage for a sign of movement. I said nothing, just followed the direction of her eyes into the shadows of the backyard. She patted the hand dry. Turning back to the living-room, she said, 'What about Harry?'

'The bird's locked up now. It can't get out.'

'The cat,' she said. 'Look at your hand. What about the boy?'

I paused before replying.

'We're stuck with Archie for as long as we want to live in this cottage. The thing could be with us for five or six years . . .'

'That's six years of watching Harry keeps right away from it. Even in the cage, it's not safe. He could open it already, you know how inquisitive he is, he has to touch everything. It's natural. If we've got to keep the filthy creature, get it somewhere secure, away from the garden.'

But we both knew that, under the conditions of Uncle Ian's will, the cormorant must remain as part of the household, on the premises. The executor would certainly see to that. I could only assure Ann that I would reinforce the wire mesh of Archie's cage or erect a second barrier to deter the child from approaching the cormorant.

The tears came. She sobbed like a child for the death of her pet. When the tears dried up, she swore at the memory of Uncle Ian, a frustrated malicious pervert, she rained curses on the cormorant. Struggling to rise from the sofa, to storm through the kitchen and into the backyard, she reached for the poker as a weapon of revenge. I prised it from her fingers and replaced it by the fireside. She breathed deeply, some colour returned to her lips. I held her close.

'Tomorrow I'll fix the cage. Don't worry now . . .'

We went upstairs. Harry was sound asleep, his cheeks rosy pink, his little blond head framed in the whiteness of the pillow. Outside, the night was still mild, a gentle December after the bitterness of the November frosts. All was quiet: no wind, no rain, no traffic, only the village which hugged itself to sleep under the slopes of Snowdon. We went to bed. Ann called out for the cat in the last seismic efforts of lovemaking. I watched the grimaces of her face in the half-light, saw the tears run into her mouth and onto the lines of her throat. She gripped me hard, I loved her with all my strength. She released a long sigh, a whisper broke from her chest. She shuddered and was still. Together we lay in the hot confusion of our sheets. With my hand I wiped a bubble of saliva from her lips, leaving a trace of blood from my injured fingers. Ann moved away, touching me unconsciously, like a young animal . . .

'Wake up, wake up! Look, it's Harry . . .'

I sat up with a start at Ann's frantic whispers, and rubbed my eyes. A moon had risen, filling the bedroom with a strong blue light. We were wide awake and watching the little figure, pyjama-clad at the foot of our bed. The child was oblivious to us. Harry had come from his cot in the next room, walked to the window, to stare into the garden behind the cottage. He did not turn towards us, even with the commotion of our waking. With his hands on the sill, he leaned forward to peer down into the backyard. Moonlight bathed his face. His eyes narrowed a little at the gleam. Harry concentrated on his object in the yard.

We crept up behind the child. Still Harry was unaware of us. We looked over him, at the blue-black garden, the purple shadows. The cage was lit by the light of steel.

Archie too was awake. The cormorant stood in the full silver beams of the moon, head and beak erect, wings outstretched. Utterly motionless. Utterly black. Not a tip of a feather trembled. It was an iron statue, a scarecrow. It was a torn and broken umbrella, a charred skeleton.

Father and mother and child stared at the bird. Harry suddenly hissed loudly, forcing the air like steam. He reached out his right hand and touched the window-pane. With the passage of a heavy cloud, the garden was in darkness. When the sky became clear again, when the cage was washed with moonlight, Archie had gone.

There was no statue, no skeleton. No cormorant.

Harry turned from the window. He walked between us as though we were invisible to him, into his own room, and clambered onto the cot. We followed and saw the child tug the blanket over him. In a second, he was sound asleep.

He slept soundly until morning.

Ann and I did not.

THREE

Ann was a formidably determined young woman. When she declared that she was leaving with Harry, going to the safety of her mother's for at least a fortnight so that the boy would forget the cormorant, there was nothing I could do or say that would change her mind. I argued that Archie would be completely secure behind strong wooden bars, that I could clean and feed the bird without releasing it, that I would never take it out for exercise except when the child was asleep upstairs. None of this was enough. Harry's moonlit communion with the cormorant had shaken her. For a few minutes, possibly longer if the child had been at the window before we had awoken, Archie had been more important to Harry than we were. He had watched and signalled to the cormorant, oblivious to our presence in the room. Ann said she would go back to the Midlands for two weeks and return to Wales for Christmas. In that time, I would be able to make suitable arrangements in the bird's routine, make the cottage a safer place for our son.

I drove Ann and Harry down to Caernarfon, where they were booked on the coach to Derby. In spite of my efforts with water and sponge, I could not disguise the smell of the bird in the little van. I swept out the dry droppings and discarded feathers, wiped the windows which were smeared by the bird's breath and tongue. But the van smelt of Archie. It had pecked holes in the plastic upholstery, pulled out beakfuls of foam rubber, leaving the seats pock-marked, pitted with yellow craters. Under the matting there was sand. A few strands of seaweed clung to the seat belts, there were fish scales like sequins which had come from the cormorant's feet. Ann rode in silence, with her face near to the open window. She held on to Harry, in the absence of a child's seat; I felt the tacit criticism, that I had adapted the van to accommodate the bird but never thought to fit a seat for the safe keeping of our son. Harry also sat silent, round-eyed, his nostrils twitching at the strong scents. Throughout the twenty-minute journey, he made no sound. He was alert to the presence of the cormorant.

In the main square of Caernarfon, we awaited the arrival of the express coach. It was a mild, damp afternoon. The lights came on in shop windows and banks, there were slippery leaves on the pavements from the young sycamores. Over and around the walls of the castle, the gulls circled, screaming. There was a mantle of droppings, like early snow, on the statues of Lloyd George and Sir Hugh Owen; the bronze figures shook their fists furiously at the birds. Harry squirmed in Ann's arms. She was glad that he was aroused from his trance, once again just a fidgeting toddler. He pointed and shouted at the people in the bus queue. Some of them smiled, others looked away, embarrassed. When the coach drew up, I kissed Ann on the mouth, wanting her to stay so much that I would have killed that wretched bird if she had asked me to. I was engulfed by my love for her; just for a moment it obliterated everything else. Harry wriggled away when I tried to kiss him, putting up a chubby fist and slapping me on the lips. They boarded the coach. As it pulled out of the square, Ann's face was close to mine through the perspex. The child was staring over my head. For a second, again there was the mesmerised glitter of dreams on his face. Harry gaped into the distance, his mouth fell open, his right hand came up and was planted on the window. The bus moved out. I shivered at the final impression of the child. Harry was pointing, gesturing wildly over my head, vainly trying to make his mother see, as the bus disappeared around the corner. When I turned, there was nothing which should have fascinated the child so much: no fire engine, no brass band, no soldiers in uniform. Only a few pedestrians on a glistening pavement, no-one familiar. Except . . . no, a grey figure, the figure of an elderly man vanishing into the warmth of a shop. I found myself shivering again. I followed the man, stopping at the shop window. And with a shrug, I saw a complete stranger, a greying stranger, rather blurred in the smoke of a dying cigar.

I drove back to the cottage in the mountains. I had already

decided that, in the absence of Ann and Harry, I could spend the fortnight trying to soothe the spirit of the bird rather than simply confining it more strictly. First of all, it would be freed from its cage, to wander on the length of its leash within the yard and garden. Archie had never shown the slightest inclination to fly: indeed, I doubted whether it was capable of doing so. Probably there had been more lasting damage as a result of its oiling in the Sussex Ouse than anyone had realised. Although it spent a great deal of energy in the boisterous flapping of its wings as a means of threatening a potential hazard, the bird never looked like leaving the ground. Therefore, even on the end of a length of washing-line, the cormorant could not go beyond the limits of the garden. It was unable to flap onto the fences which separated the yard from the neighbours' gardens. But Archie would be free to explore as far as the stream and swim in the pool at any time. There was no cat or child at risk. Perhaps the bird would surprise one of the rats which visited from the nearby farmyard.

Furthermore, I had determined that Archie would accompany me without the leash on our outings to the coast or to the quarry. I was sure that the bird would stay close. It remained dependent on me for its feeding, relying on the plates of cat food even after an afternoon's fishing for dabs.

So, that evening, in the darkness, I removed one of the panels of wire mesh from the cormorant's cage. It would be able to come and go at will, to return to its bedding of straw when the cold began to grip in the late afternoons. Archie emerged, blinking at the light from the kitchen window. I put down the tin plate and went back into the cottage. The cormorant was at large in the garden, just as it had been when the cat had gone into the gloom and met the stabs of a weighty beak. Later, before I went up to bed, I checked that Archie was secure. It was breathing evenly under a heap of straw. And in the light of early morning, the gulls came. I pulled close the curtains and slept, with the tumultuous cries surging at my window like the surf on a shingle beach. I would not be a party to the cormorant's magnetism. When I awoke again, the gulls were silent, as though they had been dismissed.

I took the bird to the quarries at Nantlle that afternoon, for its first taste of real freedom. Perhaps I should admit that I was looking forward to the two weeks on my own, to see what could be made of the cormorant. The quarries would be better than the beaches for the initial attempt at giving Archie its head: there would be no distracting people. I carried it up the winding staircase of slate and deposited it on the grassy track on top of the grey mountain. On the way, Archie had waved its bill uncharacteristically close to my face, so I was relieved to put the bird down. I was nervous, and possibly my apprehension was transmitted to Archie. When I bent to untie the slip knot from around the cormorant's ankle, it snaked at my hands, reddening the skin with a nudge of the beak. There was no blood drawn, but an aching contact of bone on bone, the sort of dazzling pain which is felt from a blow on the fleshless surface of the shin. I swore, put up my arm to fend off the bird's face, stood up and stepped smartly aside when the knot was free, seething and rubbing my fist. Very angry, I strode away towards the empty buildings. As I coiled up the rope, I walked and listened for the sound of the pursuing bird. Archie stretched the tattered wings before springing along behind me. When I turned to look, the cormorant was coming, calling breathlessly lest it lose sight of the green wellingtons.

I went from room to room with my hatchet, determined to behave as though there was no bird. I worked at the floorboards and skirting, carting it back to the manager's office where the telephone sat in one corner. There, I chopped the wood into smaller pieces suitable for kindling and easily packed for the return trip down the steps. I had a rucksack which I filled with the fuel. Deliberately shutting out any thought of Archie, I concentrated on the job until I had amassed enough wood to make the expedition worthwhile. The light was fading fast. In the shattered old buildings, the gloom fell like a curtain of purple velvet. There was no sound of the cormorant. I stood still and listened. Somewhere, a door was banging in the wind. A few twigs fell into the grate, the ruin of a jackdaw's nest. Otherwise, there was silence.

Taking up the rucksack and the length of washing-line, I went out of the manager's office and into a long corridor which gave onto a number of other doors. Now it was very dark. It was a mistake to work too long and mistime the passage of dusk in the

December afternoon. I wished I had brought a torch with me, but felt that I knew my way around the abandoned building. Stopping sometimes to listen, I stepped slowly from room to room. With the rucksack on my back, I could feel with both hands at the frames of the doorways, find my way into each little office or kitchen. I instinctively ducked to avoid hitting my head on any sagging lintel, calling softly for the bird and clicking my fingers. A rat sent up the dust from an empty room. It was silent again. But when I felt another rat brush past my legs, scrabbling with its feet to get a purchase on the smoothness of my wellingtons, I must have jumped in alarm. I heard my own voice cry out sharply just before I cracked the top of my head on a jutting slate. The darkness was filled with an explosion of shooting stars. Both hands went to my skull, the fingers feeling for blood. A prodigious pain . . .

And outside, among the rusted wheels of the quarry, the mounds of unwanted slate, only the second-hand luminosity of the street lights in the village below gave any definition to the relics of the mine. A breeze moved the heads of the dry nettles. The willowherb trembled.

I stood still in the enveloping shadows, waited for the fireworks in my head to subside.

And then there was a sound.

From along the corridor, the tread of footsteps.

'Archie?'

Something shifted the remains of a rotten floorboard, back in the manager's office which I had left behind. My head throbbed and another flare went off before my eyeballs. I turned carefully and faced along the corridor.

'Archie? Come on, Archie . . . come on . . .'

I strained to see into the gloom. Something was moving towards me, picking its way among the debris. Not the pattering of rats, a weightier tread, irregular and halting over the uneven floor, working its way closer and closer.

'That's it, Archie . . . come on . . .' I hissed into the shadows.

And the footsteps came on.

Heavier and heavier, crushing the dried-up splinters, scuffing the layers of dust. Louder and louder, the footsteps increased their pressure and volume somewhere within the spangled recesses of my skull. Involuntarily, as they bore down the corridor, I screwed my eyes tightly shut, saw another shooting star blaze across the darkness, and I stepped to one side . . .

The footsteps went past me, slowly, inevitably, over the rubble of plaster, along the corridor, fading and fading until once more there was only a rumbling, electric silence.

I remained still. I was frozen in stillness.

Until the cormorant cried from the yard outside.

I shuddered myself awake and burst from the building. There was Archie, shaking a cloud of dust from its wings.

I breathed deeply the freshness of the night. I sucked in the cold air. I gulped and sucked and gasped, to erase from my nostrils the clinging scent of a dead cigar.

From that time, there was no question that Archie could be trusted to follow me without the leash.

I stumbled past the bird and along the rough, grassy track to the top of the flight of slate steps. Down I went in the treacherous darkness, down the steps as quickly as possible without waiting or turning for the cormorant. At the bottom, I tore the rucksack from my back, flinging it with the hatchet into the van, and I leapt into the driver's seat. My hands on the steering wheel were moist and clenched; the knuckles stood up white in the glare of the street lamps. There was no traffic through the village, nobody walking the pavements. I sat in the van under the orange lights. Above me there loomed the mountain of slate, tufted with the feathery silhouettes of rowan. In the daylight, a colony of herring gulls scavenged there. Now, in the wet blackness, it was silent and still. I breathed deeply and studied the backs of my hands, the dust from the quarry offices, the sweat of my race down to the van, the wounds inflicted by Archie. The crown of my head was thudding.

The village slept.

And then the tapping on the door.

Bone against metal. The cormorant was there on the pavement, ringing its beak on the van door. Before I could get out and open up the back (for I did not want to share the cab with the bird), Archie was working to a panic of impatience. It beat the black wings. It reared up, goose-like, to rap on the window. Hoarse cries clanged along the empty street as the bird threw its tantrum. So I waited. I would not jump to attention for Archie, like a flunky, opening the doors of the car like a liveried chauffeur. Until a few lights began to appear in the upstairs rooms and porches of the terraced cottages, I waited and allowed the cormorant to exhaust its anger. Or was it afraid? Ashamed of my own retreat from the quarry, my overwhelming urge to reach the security of the van, I got out. As soon as the back doors were opened, Archie sprang up and folded its wings. We drove back, over the winding road from Nantlle, and stopped outside the cottage. Archie went unhesitatingly to the white crate, once I had attached the line to its ankle again. This time, the bird stood still, it allowed my hands on its feet, ignored my face close to its own. There was no threatening gesture of the beak. Archie disappeared into the box with a few seconds' shuffling and the rearranging of its angular limbs.

I too slept.

Without doubt, Archie was dependent on me. The length of rope was not necessary on our expeditions. For the first time, the cormorant swam free on the Menai Straits as I collected wood on the shore. It set off from the beach in determined fashion, as though late for an appointment, swimming low in the water, the beak tilted slightly upwards. Away from the land, it began to dive, shooting smoothly from the surface, clear of the water for a split-second, before vanishing without a ripple. Thirty seconds later, I saw the bird reappear. Through my binoculars, I watched the struggle with the dabs, the manner in which Archie tossed them this way and that before it was ready to begin swallowing. Then the working of the throat. Eels were brought writhing to the surface. They coiled themselves around the cormorant's bill, defying it to lure them into the rapacious gullet. A big eel wound itself with the snake-neck of its attacker, and Archie was forced to dive again to get free of its sinuous opponent. I watched and I gathered fuel. I trod among the seaweed-slippery rocks, the litter of dead crabs. Lights came on along the further shore of Anglesey. So I sat and saw the sun go down behind the trees of Newborough warren, the gulls rising from the dunes. Behind me, the castle was no longer floodlit in the evenings, for all the tourists had gone. It rose like a boulder from the harbour side, alive with the roosting of jackdaws and starlings, the hysterical laughter of gulls. They too became quiet. Archie came up on the beach, suddenly clumsy on the stones in comparision with its effortless diving, stumbling towards me through the twilit cold. It was holding something in its beak. Together we returned to the van. I put down my collection of wood.

'What is it, Archie? What've you got?'

The bird waddled forward and held up its bill to me. I instinctively withdrew my hands. In the half-light, I could not be sure what Archie was carrying, and I would never really trust the hooked beak. Archie craned forward again and put down a fish by my green wellingtons. It was a dab, still alive and convulsing, its gristly body arched with cramp. I bent to pick it up.

'Thank you, Archie. Thank you very much.'

All the way home, the fish kicked on the floor of the van. Archie stood on the passenger's seat, watched the hedgerows lit in the headlamps, the trees which fled from the passing of the car. It blinked at the lights of oncoming traffic. Once again the vehicle smelt of the bird. There was weed on the mats, the slime of eels on the windows. Archie left its signature in shit on the upholstery.

And in the house, only the second time since its arrival in the white wooden crate, Archie came into the living-room. I banked up the fire. I was still cold from the seashore, my feet ached when I took off my boots. The lights of the Christmas tree sparkled in their corner, the flames from the dry and salty log spat upwards to the chimney. Archie stood before the fire, its wings held out a little way from its chest, not stretching them, but draping them out like a fashion model in a Parisian cloak. I put down newspapers to avoid having stains on the rug. But the cormorant slept in the warmth, still standing, its wings mantled and its head turned downwards onto its breast. It slept, while the room was filled with the scents of the Straits. A little steam arose from its plumage and from my thick, woollen socks. My own head began to nod. In the warm room, Archie and I were asleep.

When I awoke, the cormorant was no longer there. I sprang up and shouted, shivering suddenly from the memory of a dream and glancing at the dying fire. I must have been asleep for hours. In my dream, there had been a frantic pursuit down the slippery staircase of the quarry: something, some grey presence was behind me, there were heavy, relentless footsteps, the whiff of smoke in the dark air . . . But then I was awake, trembling a little in my stockinged feet before the embers in the grate. And Archie had vanished.

Again I heard my voice cry out. The bird appeared at the doorway from the kitchen. It had retrieved the dab which it had given to me on the harbour front at Caernarfon, and which I had subsequently wrapped in paper and put in the dustbin. Archie came into the room to meet me, with the fish held in its beak.

'What the hell have you got there? Here, give it to me, let's put it back in the bin. I don't want to seem ungrateful, but . . .'

The cormorant allowed me to take the dab, followed me through the kitchen and into the backyard. In its search for the fish among the other rubbish, Archie had strewn the yard with pieces of paper, the broken sections of cardboard boxes, discarded vegetables.

'Bloody hell, Archie . . .'

I stooped to recover the debris. This time, I put the dead fish at the very bottom of the dustbin. But the bird's determination to offer its prize to me had given me an idea. We returned to the front room. I closed the door to the kitchen and resuscitated the fire with more logs. Some gentle music on the radio, the twinkle of the lights on the Christmas tree; the black cormorant, sea-scented, staring into the flames.

'Here, Archie, have a look at this . . .'

The bird snapped from its daydream, drawing its eyes from the golden caverns of the burning logs. It turned its face to me, numb from the heat. I had found the little collar which Ann had once bought for the cat, a flimsy thong just strong enough for a kitten. Sitting on the edge of the sofa, I reached out for the cormorant and put the collar around its neck, adjusting it to the diameter of the bird's throat and marking the leather with my thumbnail. With scissors, I made a couple of new holes in the collar and tried it again. Archie was submissive in my hands, mesmerised by the fire, standing still with wings relaxed, like a gentleman being measured by his tailor. The collar fitted snugly, neither too tight for Archie to swallow nor slack enough to slip downwards. The cormorant craned to reach it with its beak, but could not. It brought up one foot and scratched vigorously at the collar for a few moments. Then it turned once more to its scrutiny of the fire, stunned by the flames. The bird forgot the collar, as it had forgotten the cat which had worn it.

And that left a week for fishing, a week before Ann would be back with Harry. I had to go into Caernarfon to do all the Christmas shopping, and I took Archie on every trip. There were presents to buy, food and drink. I left the cormorant in the van while I went from shop to shop, wanting Ann to be pleased when she came back, impressed that I had made such an effort to prepare for Christmas instead of tinkering at the typewriter or playing with the wretched bird. I found a special gift for her, a slender gold necklace with a dangling butterfly which would flutter prettily at her throat. And a sackful of presents for Harry, things which clanked and whistled and chimed, things to occupy his mischievous fingers and distract them from the ornaments on the mantelpiece. I queued in the off-licence, wrote a disconcertingly big cheque, staggered out with my burden of Christmas spirit. Meat and vegetables, fruit and dates and nuts: more cardboard boxes to squeeze into the van. Each time I returned, Archie battered at the windscreen. It tried to spring from the van but I forced it back. As usual, people stopped to stare, aghast at the big bird beating the windows of the little car. I smiled at the spectators and answered their questions politely: no, it wasn't a goose; yes, it was quite tame but don't go too close; it was a cormorant, but no, sir, I didn't have a licence . . . until the shopping was done for the day. Then I changed into the green wellingtons, put on my waterproof jacket, took out the length of rope and attached it to Archie's ankle. The leather collar was in place around the bird's throat. Keeping the cormorant close to my feet, I led it over the swing bridge, along the sea front away from the castle, and dropped down to the stony beach. A few people paused in their walking to watch me and the bird. I let the bird have more slack on the rope, went to the water's edge. The tide was coming in over the sand flats, creeping into the channels of the estuary, licking with its creamy tongue at all the dry clumps of weed, the salt-encrusted rocks. It was midday, mid-December, with more of a bite in the air, a taste of frost. It would be colder soon, the sky was bruised. The cormorant stepped gingerly through the high-water line of seaweed, bottles, whitened spars, and came to the sea. The line was secure, the collar too. Archie floated out, miraculously transformed from the clumsy goose to a purposeful, menacing submarine. I paid out the rope and the bird began to fish.

'Go on, Archie. Get busy . . .'

The cormorant dived. For half a minute, there was nothing but the secret trembling of the rope in my hands. Somewhere in the brown water, decked in silver bubbles, with a stream of mercury pouring from the horny bill, the bird jinked and swerved in pursuit of fish. Using wings and feet as power, flying through the water, Archie was hunting. Before the shriek of the jets had ever shaken the sky over the Straits, before the churning of sand by the propellers of fishing boats, long before the first arrows sped around the battlements of the castle, Archie had been twisting through the tides of the estuary. The dabs fled, as they always fled, raising up the puffs of sand. Eels wriggled in the hope of reaching the safety of deeper water, they flashed a little grey metal and made for the shadows. In the air, the black-headed gulls circled petulantly and wondered at the world of the rumbling depths. Oyster-catchers whistled among the boulders of the shore. A pair of crows went overhead to the further land, to search the pools for the crusts of a cuttlefish. The jackdaws ate chips and crumbs in the castle courtyard. Archie was lost to the open air of the Menai Straits, connected to my hands by the twitching rope. I waited and watched the sea for the reappearance of the cormorant.

And when the narrow, black head surfaced, it was gripping the slimy sides of a dab. I saw its flatness, the size of a child's hand. Archie was fighting the fish, wrestling it, manoeuvring it, to bring it round to face the entrance of the throat. I drew in the line, very slowly. Archie continued to juggle the dab, while I took in the line and the bird was pulled towards the beach. Quicker and quicker, and the cormorant approached the shallow water. I went in to the top of my boots, winding the rope around my arm until I could reach forward and seize the bird firmly by the neck. Still Archie was preoccupied with the dab; it seemed oblivious to the rope around its ankle, even to the grip of my hand. The collar constricted its throat just enough to prevent the fish from sliding down. I dumped Archie on the beach and snatched the dab from between its jaws. By the time the bemused bird had found its bearings, peering round at me and again at the water, the fish was in the pocket of my jacket.

'Good lad, Archie, you daft bird! Go on, try again. There are lots more out there . . .'

Casting a glance at the movement of my jacket pocket, the bird turned back towards the sea and paddled away. I paid out the rope with one hand and felt for the writhing fish with the other. From behind me, on the sea wall, there came a little dry applause, some spectator impressed by my feat. I did not look round, being busy with the tangles of line in the rocks and about my boots, but I managed to take the dab from my pocket and wave it in the air above my head. The clapping became brisker, slowed down and stopped. The fish went into the bag which I had brought with me. By the time I turned to the sea wall, there was no-one there watching, only a few children cycling by.

'Well done, Archie, you clever bugger!'

I was thrilled. The bird disappeared under the water.

Time and again, over the course of the afternoon, the cormorant surfaced with a fish. And I towed it into the shore. In a couple of hours, the bag was nearly full, with sixteen or seventeen dabs; it wriggled with the mucous exertions of the dying fish. By four o'clock, Archie was exhausted. I carried the bird under one arm and held the bag of fish with my other hand. With the wet rope coiled around my shoulder, I walked back to the van. Archie sat in the crook of my arm, panting. Nobody watched as the collar was removed. From the bag I took the four eels which Archie had caught and fed them to the bird, knocking their heads on the bumper of the van first of all, to make it simpler for the tired cormorant. They rapidly vanished. The light was fading under the beetling sides of the castle.

'Great work, Archie. You can keep us in flatties for the rest of your career. It's a deal, OK, eat as many eels as you can catch, hand over the dabs to me, and we'll forget about your board and lodging . . .'

We went again to the river mouth at Caernarfon. It was better than ratting in the Nantlle quarries. In any case, I did not want to return there. In a few days, Ann would be home with Harry and perhaps I would not be able to get away fishing. So I thought it best to make the most of this new hobby, hunting with the cormorant. It was gloriously plebeian. As a schoolboy, I had often dreamed of possessing a falcon, learning the ancient laws and traditions of falconry. Now I was reaping pocketfuls of flatfish from the mudbanks of the Menai Straits, seizing them from the beak of the cormorant, alive with bone and gristle. They made a delicious soup, rather coarse and grey, but marvellous with pepper and brown bread. The van stank of fish. My hands were raw from the cold, the salt water and the inevitable contact with Archie's beak. In the cottage kitchen, there hung the clinging steam of fish broth. And I loved it all, the rusticity of it. I drove the bird from the mountain village to the coast, and I smiled when I thought how I had changed in the few months since leaving the Midlands. What would my old headmaster say if I were to meet him, by some absurd coincidence, in the harbour car park in Caernarfon? I was used to wearing a jacket and tie for school: here I was, parking a smelly van on the quayside, stepping out in tattered jeans and wellington boots, in such an ancient pullover that big holes had appeared under both arms in spite of Ann's repeated attention, in a waterproof spotted with fish scales and containing in one pocket the corpse of a forgotten flatfish; to crown the effect of such scruffy clothing, on opening up the back of the van, a dangerous, black villain of a bird would spring out, a cross between a raven and a pelican but most closely resembling a vampire bat (redolent of fish). And the hunt for food: taking the bird with its leash and collar, filling a bag with fresh fish, while other people stood stupidly in a supermarket queue. My beard had improved, I thought: instead of being closely razored under my chin and on my cheeks, I had left it to crawl over my throat and disappear below my ears. The fingernails, which were once so immaculately filed and cleaned, were now neglected. With a frown, I remembered that I had hardly added to my notes for the book during the past week, something I should return to when the business of Christmas and the New Year was over. Meanwhile, I was enjoying the raffish company of the cormorant.

Leaving the boxes of shopping in the van, once more I walked the bird from the castle, over the bridge and down to the beach. It was high tide. There was a choppy sea driving into the Straits, tossing its white crests a hundred yards from the shore and spitting spray when the waves ran against the wooden piles of the jetty. The wind forced the seas along, threw the taste of salt into my beard. I licked my lips and fastened my jacket. It was a raw afternoon. The beach was deserted and the sea wall was empty of pedestrians and cyclists. Nevertheless, Archie braced itself in the breeze, allowing its wings to fall partly open and flutter. The bird seemed as eager as ever to get into the water, so I checked the knot around its ankle and fitted the collar. My hands were a little blue already. I nudged the cormorant away with my boot, unwinding all the rope until it lay around my feet in the grey boulders. Then I jammed my hands deep into pockets, my shoulders hunched against the cold. To me, the sea looked utterly uninviting: it was whipped to a brown cream, it was angry, unhealthy, the white spume scratched from the surface and spent in the bitterness of the afternoon. But Archie set off. The line uncoiled itself. The cormorant looked lower in the water than usual, lost sometimes in the chop and spray. Splendid . . . the specialist hunter unperturbed by the conditions, a pitiless mercenary sent into the field. There was something so icily efficient about the bird, cutting through the waves on a day when the gulls and the crows had sought the shelter of the castle walls. It went down, disappeared from sight. The rope paid out.

'Good boy, Archie. Do your stuff . . .'

I turned away from the water, to have my back to the wind. There was nobody walking, it was too cold. The wind tugged at my trouser legs and blew up the hair on the back of my head.

'Bloody hell . . .'

I was thinking of the cosy cottage living-room, the log fire, the scent of the Christmas tree and the wood smoke. There would not be much fishing today, however much Archie was enjoying it. Just a few dabs, enough to thicken up yesterday's soup, and some eels for the hunter. I turned to the sea again, squinting into the wind. I could not see the bird.

'Come on, come on, it's freezing out here . . .'

But I knew it would be murky below the surface, a maelstrom of mud and sand, an underwater haboob. At any moment, Archie would reappear, after an unsuccessful chase. Maybe today there would be no dabs. I would at least have exercised the bird, it would have to eat cat food when we got home. No sign of Archie. The rope was slack about my feet. I reluctantly withdrew my hands from my pockets and bent to pick it up. As I did so, the line began to show above the surface of the water, well downstream, towards the jetty at the mouth of the river. The current had taken the cormorant nearer to the castle. I wound in the line, turning it around my wrist. It grew taut. The rope went away to my right and entered the water quite close to the slimy pillars of the jetty. I pulled tighter. It would not budge.

Quickly striding along the shore towards the bridge over the estuary, I coiled in the line, winding it around my forearm. I broke into a run when I saw the rope disappear into the coffee-coloured sea where it swirled in the legs of the pier. I leaned on the rope, my whole weight on the slender line, until it sang in the cutting wind and the droplets of sea flew from it. The bird was caught somewhere in the currents, with the rope around its ankle, the rope snagged among the weed and slime and barnacles of the wooden columns.

'Archie, Archie, you bugger . . . where the hell are you?'

Uncoiling the line again, I ran up to the sea wall, vaulting onto the promenade, and sprinted to the jetty. There was an iron gate whose sign forbade entrance to the pier, except to authorised persons. I sprang over and went to the end, trailing the slack line behind me. Then I was directly over the spot where the rope slid into the water. I wound it in and leaned out, fifteen feet above the sea, with the line taut in both my hands. I strained to see. The tide came forcing up the river mouth, throwing back the feeble currents of the river itself. Around the wooden pillars, where they sank beneath the surface, the eddies coiled and hissed like serpents. Bubbles of brown foam were sucked into the whirlpools. Again I leaned on the rope and pulled it upwards with all my strength, until I thought it gave an inch. The water writhed. If the cormorant was there, it was fighting for breath, seeing its own spark extinguished in every silver bubble which burst from its beak.

I threw off my waterproof jacket, snatching the clasp knife from its pocket. Having tied the rope to the railings of the pier, I began to clamber over the barrier, to negotiate a descent through the slimy pillars. Outwards I leaned, looking down between my legs for every footing. There were big iron bolts to grip and to stand on, icy cold to the touch, laden with grease. The wind raced through the stanchions, by my face the rope quivered. Step by step, I made the precarious descent to the surface of the water, stood there with my arms wrapped around the wet wood, breathing heavily. There was no time to spare. Bracing myself against the cold, I stepped down further, the green boots feeling for the next foothold in the racing water. Down and down, with the water now at my knees, at my thighs, while I groped for another step, tugging at my waist and sinking bitter teeth into my stomach . . . the currents around my chest . . . the breath squeezed out of me . . . I gasped and clung to the jetty, there was nowhere further for me to go . . .

Gripping fast, I felt down the rope, first with my hand and then touching the tautness of it with one boot. I plunged my face into the water, one finger pressing my glasses hard against my nose. Again I ducked my head, the aching cold throbbed in my temples and at the base of my neck, my pullover was weighted with green ice. I leaned down as far as I could with the knife in my left hand and began to saw at the rope. But I knew it was no good, that the currents and the struggles of the bird must have wound the line around the pillar, in and out of the seaweed-slimy bolts of the stanchions, that in straining on the line, in my panic, I must have tightened the tangle of knots, that even the inches it had given from my vantage point above the water were only a clenching of the knots. I worked with the knife. The rope gave. It flew from the surface with the release of tension and dangled from the railings above. But below the water, a boiling of currents gripped at my boots. The rest of the line was fast. And Archie was down there, with the rope around its ankle, among the netted cord.

I began suddenly to shake with the cold. In front of my face, I saw my own hands, blue and bruised, somehow distant, like someone else's hands. The knife dropped from my fingers, sank into the sea. I felt that I could only stay there, chest deep in the water, that I would be content to wait there, it was too much trouble to raise my heavy boots, the wood and the iron were too cold, I could not make the effort to shift my grip, it was all too complicated, too difficult . . . But, in spite of myself, my knees came up and my feet searched for a higher step. The blue hands went like spiders up the column and found a hold on the jutting bolts. When my waist was clear of the surface, the wind attacked me, seeing me exposed in my streaming clothes. The green boots emerged, glistening, slow, sea-slugs. I crooked my knees to let the water pour out, continued climbing. My eyes came level with the planks of the pier. A few more steps and I was there, leaning on the railing before swinging myself over and collapsing in a heap by the jacket I had left behind. And there I lay, with my eyes shut, with the water running from me, with the grey light of a raw afternoon draining to the gloom of evening.

I must have passed out, exhausted.

For when I awoke, it was twilight. The wind had dropped. I stood up and felt the excruciating ache of cold through my body. Everything was still, the tide had turned and the surface of the water was silken black. There was no disturbance of the inky river. It was a clear, starlit evening. I knew that I must quickly get home and out of the wet clothes, into the bath. Throwing on my jacket, I trudged to the end of the jetty and painfully heaved myself over the gate. The path along the sea wall was deserted. There was nobody on the bridge as I crossed over. Hardly any cars were parked on the quayside, the castle was not lit. It seemed that the town was empty. It was a place of silence. My own footsteps, the squelching of water in my boots, were the only sound beneath the towering walls of the castle. I shuddered and walked on, spotting the van near the edge of the harbour, leaving my trail of wet footprints and sea water dripping from my clothes. The keys were in my pocket. The blue fingers felt for them, still numb from the touch of the sea-smooth wood and the iron bolts. I took out the keys. The jangling of metal broke the silence.

At the sound, Archie stepped from the other side of the van.

I halted. For a moment, the bird stood still, its wings folded. The cormorant and I waited in the twilight. Neither of us moved.

'Archie?'

And the bird came forward.

It waddled at first, then it stretched the black wings and sprang along on slapping feet. Archie covered the yards in a series of flaps and leaps, stopped in front of me, beat a pair of damp wings, croaked once, and dropped some twitching thing by my green boots. It was a fish.

My voice was trembling.

'Thank you, Archie, thank you. Where the hell did you get to, you daft bugger?'

The cormorant croaked again and folded its wings. When I reached out and touched its head, I felt it was wet. Archie nuzzled my hand, as affectionate as a dog. In a spasm, the fish arched at my feet. I bent down, picked it up and put it in my pocket.

'Good lad . . .'

There was no rope around the bird's ankle. The collar was there on its throat. We started towards the van.

And from somewhere in the dark sky, there came a little dry applause. Someone, some spectator, was clapping, slow, sarcastic applause, increasing in speed and intensity, slowing, stopping. The clapping stopped.

I craned my neck and looked up at the castle. My head swam. Among the battlements, leaning over and applauding the reunion of man and cormorant, celebrating the gift of the fish, the silhouette of a man was there against the bright stars. The figure was still. No more clapping. The figure was entirely dark, until there was a movement of an arm, a hand went up to the head, and a pinprick of golden light glowed for a brief moment. My neck was throbbing, my eyes stinging with water.

The man vanished into the blackness of the battlements.

And falling through the air, as bright as a comet against the castle wall, falling, falling, falling, to disappear in a shower of sparks on the rocks of the dry moat . . . the butt of a discarded cigar.

In a stupor of cold and shock, man and cormorant drove through the outskirts of Caernarfon, into the foothills, and climbed into the mountains of Snowdonia. Archie sat on the front seat, as still as iron, like a dark ruin of twisted metal. I drove quickly at first, gripping the wheel with whitened knuckles, then began to slow down when we had left the town. Perhaps I had seen something that my son had seen, something which had mesmerised the little boy as he looked through the window of the bus in the town square. What had Harry seen in the garden that night? Was the cormorant alone in the backyard? What else was included in the inheritance? I shuddered, as I had shuddered in the crumbling offices of the quarry, as the tremor of fear had run down my spine at the sound of clapping, at the spark which tumbled from the battlements of the castle. The presence of a grey man fell over me, cold as the snow which would soon envelop the mountains.

But there remained a few days before Ann would return from Derby, when Archie would go back to the security of its reinforced cage. There could still be expeditions to fish for dabs; I would be more careful to watch the weather and tides. I felt my bones aching, the water from my clothes had run onto the car seat and onto the floor. More and more, I was shaking uncontrollably, my teeth beginning to chatter. The heater whirred at full blast, the inside of the van was warm and the windows steamed up, but, until I could get out of my clothes and into the bath, I was desolate. Faster and faster I drove. Still Archie seemed paralysed, a statue of a cormorant. Parking right outside the front door of the cottage, I struggled briefly with the key and flung myself into the living-room. The bird came lamely through, silent, numb.

I built the fire, using three fire-lighters to make a quick blaze from the gritty coal before laying a well-dried log on the top. The

bath was running. I left Archie in front of the rising flames while
I threw off my clothes and scampered into the bathroom. It was
wonderfully steamed up, I straightaway felt the soothing heat on
my face and in my chest. In a moment, after that glorious agony
of sinking into the scalding water, I lay back and allowed the heat
to creep into every fibre of my body. I submerged my head: the
chill in my skull was quenched, the ache at the base of my neck
was extinguished. I must have slept for an hour in my drenched
clothes, on the jetty. In that time, nobody had passed and noticed
me there, it was not an evening for the casual stroller. Now I
dozed in the warmth and steam of my bath.

And in my dream, I was at the graveside of another family
funeral. Looking down through drizzle-dappled glasses, I could
see my own feet in their funeral shoes, a long way away, as
though I was towering above them, a giant's-eye view of black
shoes in the wet grass. I could hear the droning voice of the
minister, familiar words which failed to drown the sound of soil
falling from a spade onto the lid of a coffin. Raining . . . it was
always raining at those family funerals. And who was it this time?
One of the innumerable aunts or uncles, a foreign cousin flown
back from Canada or New Zealand? I did not look into the grave.
I continued to study the distant feet and listen to the patter of
earth against the wood. Next to my own shoes, to my left, another
pair, bigger, wider, an old-fashioned pair of black, laced-up boots,
well polished, well used. On the heavy toe-caps, big drops of rain
stood and trembled, supported by the thickness of the polish.
They made my own feet seem slight, unimportant, the overwhelming presence of those boots. Still not looking up, I saw the
legs of a dark suit close to my legs. It was raining harder. Pools
were forming in the grass. The voice was blurred by the sound
of rain. And to my right, another pair of feet: black, webbed feet,
the cormorant standing respectfully at the graveside. I looked
into the grave. There was a tiny coffin, the coffin of a little child,
almost covered with brown mud. The rhythmic movement of the
spade, the gathering puddles . . . the voices grew, together with
the sounds of stone on stone as the spade threw in its layers of
rubble and gravel. And the coffin disappeared. The images faded
in the increasing rain, but the noises remained: the knocking, the

voices, growing and growing until I was awake and shivering in my lukewarm bath . . .

In the living-room, Archie was moving about. I could hear the blundering passage of its wings, something was knocked over with a thud, some books or a lamp. There was the sound of a car outside the front door, voices, arousing the cormorant from its fireside slumber. I heard the bird shift from perch to perch, its clumsy progress from the table to the armchair, onto the back of the sofa. Quickly I stood up in the water and reached for a towel. Without beginning to dry myself, I wound it around my waist and went through into the living-room.

Archie was wide awake, bristling like a panther. Every feather was electric with the tension of listening for the new voices. It stood bolt upright on the sofa and creaked with nerves. Someone was at the front door, a figure dimly outlined through the frosted glass. The cormorant cried and lifted its tail. A stream of yellow shit spattered across the furniture. I whirled at the bird.

'Bugger off, you bloody revolting creature, for Christ's sake! What's the matter with you?'

Wet and furious, I flung out an arm at the bird's face and caught it on the side of the beak. Archie toppled from the back of the sofa, onto the lamp which it had knocked off the table. There was a welt of blood on my hand from the impact with the cormorant's bill. The towel came loose. As I tucked it in at the waist, smearing the blood across my stomach and over the pink towel, the bird gathered itself. The head was snaking, it flailed the dagger beak. More books came tumbling down and a log collapsed from the fire onto the hearth as Archie moved over the carpet. I lashed out with my bare foot, but the bird seized a corner of the towel and sprang away with one powerful beat of its wings. Shaking with cold and uncontrollable rage, I stood there, stark naked, dripping wet, streaked with blood. The cormorant retreated to the far shadows of the room, to worry the towel as though it were dealing with a conger eel.

'Filthy bird! Fuck off or I'll kill you . . .'

The front door opened behind me.

Ann and Harry stepped into the room.

FOUR

'Christ almighty . . .'

That was all Ann said as she stood at the front door. She threw down her suitcase and reached out for Harry. He was staring into the dark, a frown dissolving from his face, his mouth beginning to form a vacant smile. The flicker from the flames of the tumbling logs was all the light, it picked up the wet whiteness of my nudity and the blood across my belly. In a far corner, something was moving under the table, some black thing was struggling with a pink and red opponent. There was the smell of fish.

'Upstairs, Harry, come on . . .'

She abandoned her case and disappeared up the stairs, the boy in her arms arching and convulsing in his efforts to see more of the cormorant. I recovered my wits. Moving the luggage so that it blocked the bottom step, I followed Ann into the deeper darkness. The bird was left in the living-room to finish its battle with the bath towel.

'Ann, what are you . . . ?'

'For God's sake, put some clothes on!' She spat at me like a cornered otter. 'What the hell are you doing down there? What's the bloody bird doing in the house? I come in, and there you are in a darkened room, stark naked, prancing around with a bloody cormorant . . .'

I found some clothes and dressed. I was still wet. Ann drew the curtains of the bedroom and turned on the light. Harry sat on the bed, wide-eyed, watching me dress. There was blood on my hand: it welled up from a blue graze and stained the clean shirt which I put on over my wet and blood-smeared stomach. Ann flung off her raincoat and began to unbutton the little boy's anorak.

'Look, Ann, I had no idea you were . . .'

'So what?' she hissed, without looking at me. 'By the look of things, it's a good job I came back a bit early. Someone ought to keep an eye on you. Leave you on your own for a week and God knows what obscene things you get up to!'

The boy's coat was taken off. She rubbed his hair gently with her hands and a few drops of rain flew onto the carpet. I stood still. I wanted, more than anything else in the world, to touch my wife and kiss her. Something rose in my throat when I looked at her tending to Harry, when I saw the angry colours of her face. I moved to her.

'Ann, look, I can explain everything. It was just unfortunate that you should . . .'

'Get down there and sort it out then! Or are we going to sit up here and let the bird have the run of the sitting-room?' She turned to the child. 'Now, little Harry, we'll go downstairs and get nice and warm and dry in a few minutes. When your naughty daddy has spanked that nasty bird . . .'

But the boy seemed oblivious to his mother's tender words. His eyes were fixed on my bleeding hand, he was alert to the shadowy movements of the creature below.

I went down the narrow staircase. I was going to have no nonsense from Archie. Already that day, with my ordeal in the water and the sinister scrutiny of our reunion, I had had enough of the bird's mischief. Prepared for a confrontation, I stepped over the suitcase at the foot of the stairs. I found the light switch. In the sudden brightness, it seemed that the room was not so chaotically upset as it had appeared in the dancing glow of the flames. The cormorant had returned to its place in front of the fire, leaving the towel in the corner.

'Right, Archie, you bugger, you're going out into the yard. Come on . . .'

I advanced, with a heavy cushion in my left hand, with the right ready to fly at the bird's throat, the best and safest hold. But Archie waddled sedately past me towards the door and waited there for me to open it. I turned the handle, the door swung open. With a haughty nod, an adjustment of the wings in the manner of a bride about to begin her progress up the aisle, Archie swept out of the room. I quickly followed, eager to take advantage of the cormorant's co-operation, and ushered it into the backyard, through the opening of the cage. The bird disappeared into the crate, buried itself among the straw. The cage was secured. I scampered in from the lightly falling rain and locked the back door behind me.

'Jesus . . .' A long sigh of relief.

Ann was already in the living-room, at work on the long squirt of shit. Harry watched the operation from near the Christmas tree. Without speaking, I picked up the books and the table lamp, whose bulb was not broken, repaired the fire and swept up the ash from the hearth.

'Come to me, Harry,' I said, and the little boy scrambled into my arms. I kissed him on the forehead and smelled the bright, clean hair.

'What've you been up to then? Been a good boy for your mummy?'

'More than we can say for you,' said Ann. She came to the sofa and sat down next to me. 'I love you, I love you,' she whispered, looking away towards the fire as though these were words she could not safely say to my face. 'You silly man . . .' And she collapsed gently backwards, to lean against my shoulder. My arm went around her waist. Without moving my head, I could inhale the scent of the woman and the warmth of the child.

'I'm sorry,' I said into the cloud of her hair. 'It's all so stupid, isn't it?' I turned her round to face me. Harry wriggled on my knee and put up a chubby hand to his mother's mouth. 'But what are you doing here? Why are you early? How did you get up here from Caernarfon?'

There was no mystery attached to Ann's unexpected return. A week with her parents in Derby was more than enough: she was missing her husband. She wanted to get back to the cottage and to the hills, away from the Midland suburbs. Of course, it was nice at first to be in the bosom of the family and to see some old friends, but, time and time again, she had had to reiterate the story of our unusual inheritance; and then, there were furtive looks exchanged between her listeners, who obviously doubted the truth of the tale. Why should she suddenly flee her husband and the remote Welsh village? What was the matter with the relationship? What kind of goings-on took place up in the mountains? These questions went unasked, but Ann had sensed a shiver of delicious scandal through the company of friends and neighbours, people who had raised their eyebrows months ago on first hearing of our plans to move to Wales. They thrilled to hear about the disappointments and disillusionments of rash youngsters: it made their suburban lifestyle seem more acceptable. So Ann determined to come back as soon as she could. That morning, quickly packing her single case, she thanked her parents for their hospitality, kissed them both lightly on the cheeks (mother was squeezing out a pearly tear), and took the coach from the centre of Derby to Caernarfon. And a taxi into the hills, thinking she would spring a surprise on her lonely husband.

'And what about Harry? Was he all right?'

She hesitated, touched the boy's cheek. He was tired. Soon he would go up to bed.

'Well, yes, I suppose he was all right. Only, he wasn't exactly the life and soul of the party. So Mum, of course, thought there was maybe something wrong with him, maybe we weren't giving him a very good diet, all the right vitamins and so on. Implying that perhaps I wasn't a particularly wonderful mother, like she was . . .'

'What do you mean?' I asked. 'Didn't he show off his walking, reaching out for all your mother's priceless ornaments? I imagined he'd create havoc in the midst of all that twee suburban style.'

Again she paused. On my knee, Harry was closing his eyes. He had fallen forward against my chest, his thumb in his mouth.

'No,' she said. 'I could hardly stir him off my knee. He wouldn't go to Mum or Dad, just turned away from them and stuck his face in my neck. It was weird. He'd sit for hours as we were chatting, almost like a little adult, as though he was listening politely to our conversation but was too shy to join in. I couldn't interest him in anything in the house, he didn't want to explore or to break anything. Couldn't care less about their cat.' She frowned, searching for the right words. 'You know, if he'd been a grown-up, you would've said he was boring, just sitting there, glazed, vacant . . .'

'All day? What's the matter with him?'

'Well, no,' continued Ann. 'The funny thing was that he perked up whenever I took him out, to the shops or into the park. He'd be sitting there like a doll, on the bus, or if I'd plonked him on the trolley in a supermarket, and then he'd suddenly come alive, as though he'd had an electric shock or something. Pointing wildly through the window, slapping his hands on the glass, forcing my face round to look at somebody or other. Or practically standing up on the trolley, so that I'd have to plonk him down again, waving his arms, shouting, jabbing his fingers . . . always pointing into the distance, into the crowd.'

I shivered.

'What was he looking at? Did you see anything, anybody he could have recognised?'

'Don't be silly, darling. He's only a toddler. They don't recognise people, there were just crowds of people, shoppers, pedestrians . . .'

I added nothing, remembering the child's frantic gestures from the coach in the square in Caernarfon, my own puzzled pursuit of an elderly stranger.

'And once we got home again, I mean to Mum and Dad's, he went back into his shell. Like someone had switched off his electric current. He sat on my knee like a ventriloquist's dummy, except that I couldn't make him perform. Mum and Dad got a bit huffy about it, because he wouldn't go near them and wouldn't show them how he could walk.' Ann sighed. 'So, what with all that and being cross-examined by the neighbours about you and the cottage and the village, I just wanted to come back.' She giggled and nestled up to me. 'And if they'd come in and seen you cavorting in the nude with your bloody cormorant, all firelit and gory, lost to the world in some smutty fetish . . .'

But I was not listening. I felt cold.

'Come on, my little Harry,' I said. 'Bedtime for you.'

The boy stirred in my arms. He sat up, rubbing his eyes with the backs of his hands, coming awake. He looked around the room and frowned, as though he was seeing it for the first time. His eyes were cold as pebbles. Harry squinted at Ann and then at me, dismissed us as total strangers, turned his hot little face towards the fire and sniffed the air like a dog.

'What's up, Harry?'

The child ignored Ann's question. He wriggled from my lap and set off in the direction of the Christmas tree. There was something which he wanted, which he must have. Again I found myself shivering. In the toddler's tender frame, the angle of his sparkling blond head and the unsteadiness of his gait, there was an incongruous element: the ice which formed behind his eyes.

'What are you looking for, Harry? Come on, show your mummy.'

Harry bent for a moment at the foot of the tree, then he turned around with his prize. His face was ablaze, with a grin like a gash, his eyes were splinters of ice. And he lunged at me and Ann, jabbing at us with his weapon.

It was a feather, a long, black feather, shot through with green and wet with shit.

Ann squealed and turned her face away, fending off her son with random swipes of a cushion.

'Let's have it, Harry!' I said, much more loudly than I had intended.

My voice quavered. In a second, I had the feather in my hand.

'Nasty old thing, dirty old feather. You don't want that, Harry. Let's put it on the fire.'

But it took all of Ann's efforts to restrain the child as I dropped the feather onto the flames. He wrestled and kicked, he clawed and spat and bellowed. Dry-eyed, Harry gazed at the fire as the feather was consumed. And when it was gone, in a whiff of pungent smoke, he looked at me and croaked some incoherent oath, as if he were wielding a curse in my direction. I had had enough. It was time for bed. I took him from Ann, who was holding him close to her, and delivered an old-fashioned slap across his backside.

'Have a proper cry, Harry,' I said, laughing to see him dissolve into real, spontaneous tears. It was a relief to watch him become a child again.

The three of us went upstairs. Harry was suddenly sleepy, as though the tears had spent the remains of his energy. Once he was in bed, Ann and I kissed him on his hot cheeks. The light went out and we came down once more to the fireside. I gave Ann some sherry, poured myself a glass of beer; a bit of music;

the lamp switched off; the coloured stars on the Christmas tree glinting in the glow of the flames. So I began to recount my successes with Archie, the triumphant return from the beach with the trophies of the hunt. I did not mention anything which might worry her, I said nothing of my ducking or our furtive observer.

Somehow, if the bird was ever going to be an accepted part of the household over the course of another four or five years, then both Ann and Harry should share the interest, be involved in its welfare. It was simply not feasible to have it imprisoned in the yard for months on end, like some festering prisoner in a dungeon, something to be fed and watered, something ugly from which a woman would recoil in horror. I heard my own voice, calmly persuasive, but an image kept recurring as I spoke: that picture of Harry advancing on us with the black feather, Ann flinching from the ugliness of her own son. The voice continued. I told her that Archie just happened to be in the room when she came in, because we had both come back from the beach very cold and wet (and this was true), so I had allowed the bird to warm itself by the fire while I was in the bath (which was also true). It was unfortunate that Ann's arrival at the door had thrown the cormorant into another of its tantrums. She listened carefully to my account of our fishing expeditions and smiled at the novelty. Since we were stuck with the bird, not without some very attractive advantages such as the cottage and Harry's inheritance, it would indeed be foolish to gripe about it for the coming few years. Two intelligent young people should be able to control it and even mould its presence into a worthwhile addition to our bucolic lifestyle. Maybe Harry could benefit from such an unusual companion, my voice was smoothly saying. Together, we could take a more positive attitude towards Archie, learn something, understand something from it. We loved the cottage and had settled down well in the village. Surely it was right that we should have to work to keep our new life.

I sensed my advantage as I talked. Ann was listening. It had been my greatest asset as a teacher, the ability to sound utterly reasonable, apparently to speak sense. This is not such a common talent among schoolteachers. So I planted a long kiss on Ann's upturned throat. My hands went to her breasts, undid the buttons

of her blouse, slid behind her back to the fastening of her bra. In
front of the fire, she was released from her clothing, chuckling
as I hurled each item into the corners of the room. I quickly
stripped. Lying together on the rug, we surveyed the flamelit
room: her knickers had caught on the light shade, the bra swung
gently from the typewriter, there were clothes strewn across the
furniture. So I kissed her eyelashes, her chin and her throat, and
continued to kiss her from her throat to her knees. She was
sculpted in white marble, made warm by the blaze. It threw her
into shadows and caverns of reds and blacks, places so scarlet
and hot that my tongue could taste the heat. She turned on me
so that her heavy breasts lay on my chest, she swung the nipples
across my lips and danced them on my face. I kissed her until
she squealed. She slid and worked herself onto me, to move and
work until she could only howl and collapse helplessly on my
chest. I kissed her entire body again, as though at any time I
might lose her, so that each kiss would reinforce my ascendency
over her. She closed her eyes and relaxed under the balm of my
kissing. She could not have seen what I was doing. Her body was
marked with the blood from my hand. Every tender touch against
her throat and face, over her breasts and silken stomach, among
the heat of her thighs, each caress branded her with blood. I
smeared her marble body. My whispered endearments numbed
her into a stupor. Soon she was asleep in the falling colours of
the fire, stained with the wounds inflicted by the cormorant.

All of this, so Archie might be forgiven.

There dawned one of those crisp December mornings in the
mountains, when the air is full of the scent of the fir trees, so
cold that it scalds the nostrils, humming with sunlight under a sky
of unblemished blue. Christmas was just three days away. When
I stepped into the garden, I breathed deeply and looked up to see
a pair of buzzards wheeling and diving far above me. Their plaintive
cries floated like thistledown. I squinted into the sunshine, lost
the buzzards in the brightness. A raven croaked from the hillside.
The sheep were steaming in the warmth of the direct rays,

basking in the heat after a bitter night. It was strange: I could stand in the yard and enjoy the glow of the sun on the back of my dressing-gown, yet plumes of cold blew from my mouth and nose. What a day . . . a good day not to be driving into the car park of a big comprehensive school, a good day not to be taking a double period of drama with thirty-five cynical adolescents, a perfect day not to be on duty in the cacophony of the school cafeteria. I inhaled fiercely and felt the hairs on the insides of my nostrils burning with cold, loved myself for being supernaturally lucky, went inside to the smell of frying bacon. Ann was in the kitchen, warm and sleepy in her dressing-gown. I wrapped my arms around her from behind and kissed her hair.

'That's enough of that,' she said in her teaching voice. 'Keep an eye on Harry, will you, he's in the living-room.'

The boy came tottering into the kitchen at that moment, holding two trophies of his early morning exploration: a pair of underpants and a bra.

We all laughed.

'Oh, thank you, Harry, what splendid presents!'

Ann was not expected in the pub that day, indeed until after the New Year. I proudly displayed the shopping I had already done for Christmas and earned myself a kiss for my efforts. The cottage was tidy and clean once more, the family was reunited. My suggestion that we should all go out was greeted with instant approval.

'All of us,' I said. 'All four of us.'

A momentary pursing of the lips, then, 'Yes, all right,' she said. 'I'll make some sandwiches and things for a picnic, you get Harry organised. And the bird, of course . . .'

I washed and dressed and did the same for Harry while Ann was busy in the kitchen. Then the child was occupied in the living-room with some of his noisy toys, Ann was in the bath, and I went out to the van. I sponged down the seats and the matting and made sure that the barrier which separated the back compartment from the passengers was quite secure. Fragments of fish, seaweed and feathers were all swept out into a plastic bag. I wiped the windows and sprayed a cloud of disinfectant into the van before slamming the doors closed. I went to fetch Archie.

Ann came out of the bathroom with just a towel round her. At my warning shout, she scooped up the boy and took him upstairs, as a precaution, while I came through the front room with the cormorant. It was a good start to the expedition: the bird stalked up to the van, with a gentle coaxing from the leash (especially tightened around its ankle), and flapped into the back when I opened the doors. It sneezed like a cat at the smell of the spray, but settled down in the fresh straw which I provided. I had the collar in my pocket, I had checked and re-checked the new knot in the leash. Archie was ready. I was determined nothing should go wrong to spoil the beginnings of a new understanding of the cormorant.

It was the closest that Ann and Harry had been to Archie. They sat in the front seat, every muscle tense for the first few miles, with only the wire mesh between them and the bird. When it came close and poked its beak through the holes, Ann whispered, 'Bloody hell,' and turned to look out of the window. Harry chuckled, blew a bubble, and went to bat at the beak with his hand. Ann restrained him.

'Be a good lad there, Archie,' I said over my shoulder. 'Nearly there now.' And to Ann, I added, 'The bugger's in a good mood today. Just relax, it can tell if you're frightened. It can't hurt you here, and I'll keep it right away from you and Harry when we get to the beach.'

She made a brave smile, touched my hand.

We arrived at the castle in the bright sunlight of midday. The car park was practically empty. The air was perfectly still, the tide quite high but going out. I found myself looking round and inspecting the few pedestrians, and I threw a surreptitious glance along the grey blocks of the battlements. People would be at work or queueing in the supermarkets for the rest of their Christmas shopping. Ann and Harry got out of the van. While they were admiring the swans, twenty of them which were sailing grandly among the yachts and cruisers, I opened up the back and brought out the cormorant. Tying it to the rear bumper, I organised coats and extra pullovers for my wife and son, then locked the doors. Harry was not impressed with the swans: they were too clean and respectable, perhaps. He wriggled in Ann's arms to turn and stare at Archie. Together we watched as the bird loosened its muscles, stiffened by a night in its crate and its confinement in the van. Feathers flew. The glittering air sang with the whistle of black wings. Archie stretched to the tips of its feet and lashed out its aching sinews. The gulls came from the castle walls, fell close by and wheeled away, screaming at the menace of the cormorant. Here was something, in the castle car park, attached to the bumper of a small van, which was more than the everyday sea-crows on the brown waters of the estuary. It came and went in the company of a man, not his slave, for they had seen him retreat from the wild beak, but in the company of people. It was more than the cormorants along the shore, much more than the swans which preened themselves in their muddy reflections, immeasurably more than the biggest of the black-backs or the oldest raven. The gulls swooped down to see. They recoiled from something they could not understand.

Ann and Harry, the latter insisting on walking unaided, followed at a safe distance as I went over the bridge with the bird.

While I dropped onto the beach and was busy fixing the collar to the cormorant's throat, they continued further along the sea wall to the steps which the boy could negotiate. The shingle shore was a treasure trove for Harry. Time and time again, he fell on his knees with a gurgle of delight on spotting some object which was irresistible to his teeming imagination. There were cuttlefish, the leathery eggs of the rays; stones with stripes and hoops and spots, stones which were riddled with holes or studded with barnacles; necklaces and headbands of seaweed; numerous old shoes, the skeleton of a black umbrella; green bottles, blue bottles, clear bottles and those whose glass had been scoured to swirls of milky clouds by the friction of the sands; the waterlogged corpses of gulls and pigeons, the bright orange beak of an oyster-catcher, the foot of a swan; a pair of horn-rimmed spectacles, a briefcase of good leather, locked up and containing all manner of scandalous secrets; more bejewelled boulders and emerald weed . . . the worn-out spars of shipwrecks, the flotsam and jetsam of innumerable complicated lives. Ann stayed with the boy, relieving him firmly of the least acceptable trophies but letting him comb the beach for more treasures. She sat on a dry rock and felt the

December sun fall on her hands and on her face. She tasted the salt on her lips. Quite nearby, I was standing up to my ankles in the water, the line streamed out to sea and there was the black shadow of the cormorant, motionless for a second on the sparkling tide before it dived below the surface. Ann gasped. It was beautiful. Archie was suddenly different, moving across the gentle swell and diving like a knife into the green depths. The cormorant dropped its hooliganism and went hunting; its filthy manners were nothing but an affectation. We had known boys and girls in school who had been the same, who adopted the armour of the gross and the crass, who spat and puked and blew their noses on the curtains to disguise a sensitivity which had once been highly prized. Archie performed. In the water, the cormorant was healthy, vigorous, clean.

'Go on, Archie!' Ann was calling out.

And when it surfaced, with a silver fish wriggling in its beak, she jumped up from her rock with a little cry. She called to me as I was drawing in the rope, and waved wildly.

'Wonderful!' she yelled, and I could see the welling of tears in her eyes. It had been just the same at school.

I pulled in the bird, snatched the fish from its beak and put it in the pocket of my jacket. In a moment, the puzzled cormorant was once more breasting the waves and heading out into deeper water. There was a burst of applause from behind me. I spun round, as though I had been stung by a wasp, and there was Ann, delighted at the success of our hunting expedition. Harry winced at the sound of clapping, dropping his armful of treasure onto the beach. I returned to the fishing, while Ann soothed her sobbing son.

In an hour, father and son had accumulated more prizes than we could carry. My plastic bag was full to bursting with eels and dabs, all struggling to prolong their lives by gaping their sticky mouths into the sunlight. Their bodies, writhing together in the bag, had made a mucous lather in which the fish would drown. We persuaded Harry to leave all but the most precious of his collection: he decided to keep a string of seaweed pearls and a pink shampoo bottle. From a discreet distance, Ann and Harry watched Archie enjoying the fruits of its work. I tipped the entire

contents of the bag onto the sea wall, where the fish blew bubbles
and convulsed on the dry concrete. Harry's mouth fell open in
astonishment. He mimicked the cormorant's rasping croak,
lunging forward with eager hands. Here were far better toys than
anything he could find on the seashore, jumping, skittering toys.
Ann restrained him. Having removed the collar from the cormorant's throat, I fed the eels to the bird one by one, stunning some
of them first for the benefit of the weary hunter, but offering the
others live for Archie to overpower and swallow, for the benefit
of Ann and Harry. For Ann, Archie had reverted to its loutish
manners; away from the water, it was ungainly and crude. But
she was thrilled by such gluttony. The eels slid down Archie's
throat, the pulsating bulge descended as the cormorant released
a belch of steam into the cold. Harry stared, with the solemnity
of expression which only the very young and the ancient can
achieve.

Archie was replete. We all went back to the van. I put the bag
of dabs on the floor by the driver's seat and tied the bird to the
bumper. Still the car park, under the walls of the castle, was quite
empty. It was perfect for us to sit on the harbour side and eat
our picnic. We watched the efforts of one dishevelled swan to re-
join the big group of swans in the face of nearly twenty hostile
beaks. Ann called to the birds, her teaching voice again, as though
she were sorting out some playground bullies. We both laughed
at our old school charades, the feigning of outrage or surprise
when laughter would have been appropriate. The bullying swans
ignored her. I shouted to their victim: 'What's the matter now,
Pilbury? Stop blubbing, for heaven's sake! Get stuck in there,
let's see a bit of backbone!' The swan drifted off, pecking at a
few displaced feathers. There was a Pilbury in every playground.

Behind us, Archie stood in the sunshine and held out its wings
to dry.

But a chill settled soon over the late afternoon. The moment
the sun was shrouded, we realised how cold it was. While we
were in Caernarfon, Ann wanted to have a quick look at the shops
in their Christmas splendour. I put the cormorant into the back
of the van; the bird was tired now and hopped eagerly onto its
bed of straw. I carried Harry, who was snugly wrapped in his

little anorak and peering gnomishly from inside the fur-lined hood, and Ann walked with her left hand nestling in my jacket pocket. She grimaced at the dampness of the dabs there and said I was only a silly old teacher with fish scales in my pockets. But I knew she was happy. Together we went into the town square. The lights had come on in the shop windows, there was a splendid Christmas tree strung with coloured bulbs. People were bustling from shop to shop, their shoulders hunched, their hands in their pockets, laden with parcels or children, or staring emptily into the warmth of the supermarkets. The gulls were silent under the darkening steel of the sky. Harry's nose was going red.

'Let's have a look inside, get warmed up a bit,' said Ann.

We went from shop to shop and bought nothing. The spirit of Christmas was everywhere, cheap and trivial in some places, glamorous in a few shops, appalling in others. The coming of Christmas affected everyone. Nobody was unchanged, no-one escaped. It strengthened the bonds between the happy, the lovers, the members of united families; it emphasised to the unloved and the wounded the bitterness of their plight. Ann squeezed my fingers deep in my fishy pocket, Harry planted a wet kiss on my forehead before slapping me repeatedly on both cheeks. It was so warm in all the shops. And outside it grew colder.

It began to snow. The world was changing. The square was blurred with the steady fall of large, moth-like snowflakes. They floated through the blue twilight, into the white and yellow lights of the town. People stopped walking, turning their faces away from the glare of the window displays and looked up at the sky. They put out their hands and caught the flakes, to examine them for a second on the warmth of their skin. Children were seen with their heads thrown backwards, their eyes closed, their tongues stuck out, squealing at the tingle-taste of the snow. It settled like confetti on the shoulders of the policeman and the traffic warden, caught them in conspiratorial conversation. An old man swore loudly and jammed down the brim of his cap. A single gull swam among the thistledown flakes, bigger and whiter but somehow less substantial, a ghost from the grey walls of the castle. Suddenly, someone with an eye for spectacle switched on the floodlights, bathed the ancient stones in a golden glow, coal-black shadows alive with falling snow. And the people cheered, they cheered and clapped when their castle leapt from the darkness. The magic was complete. There was snow in Ann's hair and on her eyelashes. Harry looked angry, all this was so confusing. He went cross-eyed at the impertinence of a flake which settled on the tip of his nose. I roared an incoherent roar with my beard and glasses smudged.

It was the sort of snow that settles, sticking fast to the trees and the lamp posts and the cars and to the roofs of the buildings. Sir Hugh Owen and Lloyd George were whitened with a mantle of snow, fresh and clean after their customary spattering of droppings from the gulls and the pigeons. It continued to fall heavily. Soon the square was muffled. Footsteps seemed silent, the passing taxis whispered. The voices of excited people rang eerily around the walls of the castle. There were no gulls. The jackdaws sulked among the battlements. We went carefully down the street to the harbour car park. The tide had gone out; the wet mudbanks and the remains of the river were the only places which refused the snow. Huddled together under the hull of a big yacht, the swans slept, their heads tucked under their wings. Even now, in the uncomfortable conditions, the single outcast was on its own, wide awake, shaking the snow from its feathers on an exposed sand flat.

'Poor old Pilbury . . .' muttered Ann, and she turned away to the van.

The cormorant was asleep. All the windows of the van were coated with snow, and the bird was snug among the straw and the darkness. It hardly raised its head when I unlocked the doors. Harry was weary too. He sat on Ann's knee, and his eyes began to close even while I went round and scraped the snow from the windscreen. Once we set off, the van soon became warm inside. Harry slept. Ann put her right hand on my thigh. There was no sound from the cormorant. I drove carefully, for the road was whitened with a carpet of snow and only a little traffic had passed along and left its wheelprints. Sometimes I felt that sickening second when I knew the van was beginning to slide, that feeling through my hands on the steering wheel and my backside on the seat that told me to wait and relax for an instant until the tyres bit again. Ann was unperturbed. As we climbed away from Caernarfon the snow stopped falling. The roads were clearer but the fields were uniformly white, the trees and the dry stone walls were daubed with snow. It would be colder now. The sky was clear, aching with stars. We were nearly home.

'All right, love? Is he asleep?'

'Mmm . . . he's well away,' she answered. 'A lovely day out, my darling. How did you manage to arrange for the snow as well? Is it something to do with your pagan rites with Archie in the firelight?'

'That's a secret,' I said. 'I thought you'd like it. Anyway, that's nothing. My next miracle is the fish soup. You'll love it, all caught by our very own tame fisherman.'

She nodded. 'I was impressed, I must admit. Although I still don't think "tame" is quite the appropriate word. You've got to hand it to the beast though: it can fish.'

We pulled up in front of the cottage. The village was deserted, just a few cars parked outside the pub, hardy drinkers determined to brave the weather. I went in first with Archie, while Ann stayed behind with the sleeping boy. The cormorant allowed itself to be carried from the bed of straw, although I held its neck with one hand and kept the beak turned away from my face. When I returned to the van, Ann had emerged and was standing on the pavement. Harry woke up.

'Hello, my little Harry,' she whispered, kissing his hot forehead. He was tousled and sticky from sleep. 'You're all hot and cuddly, aren't you? You've had a nice day out at the seaside, haven't you, with all your treasure hunting and those funny fishes . . .'

The child blinked at her, rubbed his eyes. He stared about him, at me, at the snow-covered roofs, at his own frosty breath. He blew a plume into his mother's face. She kissed him again.

'Look, Harry . . .'

And above our heads there stretched the oceans of stars. There were white stars, blue stars, red stars, stars of silver and gold. We strained our ears in the silence of the hills until we could hear the crackling and the splintering, the rumbling extinction of an ancient star and the tinkle of the first awakening of the brand new stars, like a breeze through the glass of a delicate chandelier. It was an ant-hill of stars. One moment they were suddenly close, pressing down against our eyeballs, so I felt I could reach up, take a handful and let them trickle through my fingers. Then they sprang away and kept on going, speeding into the purple distance.

'Look, little Harry . . .'

He looked. His eyes followed the line of Ann's pointing finger. He craned his neck. Both his hands stretched up. Here was more treasure. His day was full of treasures, it was a mystery. Some he had been allowed to take, others he had been forced to discard, the squirming ones he could not touch, and these, the prettiest of them all, were infuriatingly just beyond the reach of his fingers. So he groped for them and blew a cloud of smoke. Now his hands were cold. He put them on his mother's cheeks and leaned forward to press his face into her neck, where it was warm and soft.

We went inside. I knelt at the hearth, busy with the firelighters and coal. Ann sat the child on the sofa and began to undo his buttons, before going to the tree and turning on the Christmas lights.

'More stars, Harry,' she said.

He scrambled over to the tree, fell to the carpet and filled his fists with the fir needles which had dropped there. Soon the flames were dancing in the grate, taking the chill from the air in the living-room. While Ann was upstairs, I put on some music and poured out two glasses of sherry, setting them on the mantelpiece for when she came down again. She would be brushing out her hair in front of the bedroom mirror. I pictured her turning this way and that to catch the different angles, stroking hard with the brush until her hair was shining and alive with static. I waited for her, with the backs of my legs warming over the flames, and I hummed along with the music. Harry was engrossed with the needles, silent, preoccupied with their scent and their tingling sharpness.

Then the boy stood up. He turned away from the tree and waited, motionless, alert. The child was listening for something, something beyond the music and the crackle of the fire. And sniffing the air, his nostrils dilated. He went to the sofa and sat down.

'What's up, Harry?'

But the child was deaf to my question. His eyes did not so much as flicker in my direction. Alert, concentrating, every muscle in his face frozen, he tested the air like a hunted animal, gazed into the flickering fire.

Ann's voice came from the top of the stairs. 'You're a bit extravagant, aren't you? It's not Christmas yet, you know . . .'

She came down. I pointed to the sherry and spoke quietly, although I was beginning to understand what she had meant. 'Only a little drop, to celebrate the expedition.'

'Oh no,' she said. 'I didn't mean that.' Frowning, she looked around the room, at the table, the mantelpiece, the window sill. 'I'd love a glass of sherry, but . . .' Still puzzled, she added, 'But I could have sworn I got the whiff of one of your horrible cigars . . .'

And Harry began to laugh, an ugly croaking laugh, as he stared into an empty space.

FIVE

Christmas Day itself was raw and blustery after the earlier promise of the snow, which only remained in patches in the lee of the dry stone walls and the shelter of boulders. By the roadside, the snow had turned to a muddy brown slush: it flew up from the wheels of traffic and soiled the doorsteps of the cottages in the village. On higher ground, the scree was flecked with white, as though the hills were suddenly crowded with sheep, a big bright flock of clean sheep. There were hardly any fields of snow. It lay so thinly that the movement of the livestock and even the passage of jackdaws and pigeons had scuffed it aside. The streams had turned to torrents, silver scratches on the mountainside, like flashes of forked lightning. The water roared at the bottom of the garden. It was a white Christmas, just, but a disappointment after the heavy fall a few days before. Grey skies unravelled, like the greasy wool of the hill sheep, snagged on the tops of the Snowdon ridge, pressing on and leaving a tangle of cloud in the same way that the sheep would decorate the barbed wire with knots of fleece. Sometimes a flurry of rain rattled on the windows of the cottage. It was cold.

I got up early before Ann was awake. Very quietly, I drew the blankets aside and left her sound asleep in bed. I went downstairs, shivering in my pyjamas and slippers. Through the kitchen window, I saw the cormorant was still inside the white wooden crate, and I grimaced at the greyness of the morning. I had said nothing the previous evening to Ann's remark about the cigar. She had just looked around again, shrugged and gone to Harry. He lunged away from her, as though he would dash himself in the flames of the fire, before instantly stopping in puzzled contemplation of the blaze. It might have been the first time he had seen it, for he frowned in bewilderment and stretched out his fingers. Then he awoke from his brief trance, to smile beatifically on his mother and continue playing under the tree. I shivered again, thinking of the dim moth-like presence which had been felt by all of us, by me and Ann and Harry. A strange atmosphere for the child to grow up in, in the company of a cormorant and some shadowy philanthropist.

There I was in the kitchen at seven o'clock on Christmas morning, the only member of the household awake. I went into the living-room and set to work. Under the tree, I piled up the brightly coloured presents, most of them for Harry, but others too which had arrived by post for me and Ann. There were small gifts for Mr and Mrs Knapp, the couple who ran the village post office and shop, for they were coming to have lunch with us. I brought in a basket of logs, thoroughly dry and kept aside for the special day. When the fire was lit, I left the logs close to the hearth so they would be toasted and ready for their turn among the flames. And I began to prepare a celebratory breakfast for Ann. As I did so, busying myself by the kitchen window, I saw Archie make its first appearance of the day from its box. First of all, the crate swayed from side to side; a series of handfuls of straw flew out onto the floor of the cage; the bird's head emerged, looking infinitely surprised to be in a makeshift chicken run rather than on a jetty overlooking some exposed estuary; the neck thrust upwards, two wings hooked themselves over the edges of the woodwork; the cormorant heaved itself indecorously out of its bed, to land, sprawling on its breast, on the slates of the backyard. Archie stood up. It stretched its neck and wiggled the stiff tail-feathers. Each black foot was held out at right angles to its belly, the ankles loosened. And the *tour de force*, the slow and painful extension of the wings after a night's confinement, before they were shaken from sleep into a whirlwind of whistling plumage. Two further details of the morning ritual remained to be seen to: with the beak, so much dishevelled green and black mane had to be reorganised, and then the longest and most arrogantly arched jet of shit was squirted across the yard. The cormorant was awake.

I went out hurriedly with the bacon rind and some gristle which

I had cut from the kidneys. Archie took them gently from my fingers.

'Good boy, Archie. And a merry Christmas to you.'

I skipped back indoors. Bearing the breakfast triumphantly on a big tray, I went up the stairs and into the bedroom. I put the tray down on Ann's dressing-table, sat on the end of the bed, took both her feet in my hands as they stuck up under the blankets and began to caress them. She groaned, her feet retreated as she curled up her legs. So I shifted to the top of the bed where I could lean over and kiss her on the neck. She remained still, with my lips on her throat. Her breathing stopped. There was only a flutter of a pulse under the skin, like the movement of a moth behind a curtain. Then she breathed out slowly, her whole body relaxed, her lips parted in a luxurious smile. In a moment I was trapped within her sleepy embrace.

Breaking free, I went to the dressing-table and turned round with the tray.

'To satisfy another of your outrageously healthy appetites . . . Happy Christmas, darling.'

We kissed long and deeply, until she peeped from one eye. 'Look, it's Harry,' she managed to say into my hair, and the little boy came drowsily into our room. We scooped him up and sat him between us in the warmth of the double bed.

'Look what Daddy's got for us,' said Ann. Harry was thoroughly kissed and tickled by both of us until he writhed away into the dark caverns of the bedclothes. Together we ate the breakfast, crumbs and marmalade and spots of coffee on the sheets, Harry sucking a slice of bread which Ann had dipped into the yolk of an egg, while I, the dutiful husband, picked up the pieces of bacon and kidney which were considered too black for my wife. I climbed back into bed. Harry scrambled over us, up and over our bodies as though he were tackling an assault course. We winced at the punishment of his little hands and feet, he chuckled as he thumped us. Then we were all weary. Among the wreckage of a Christmas breakfast in bed, we slept.

And when we went downstairs, the room was warmed by the fire that I had lit at seven o'clock. It was time for Harry to open his presents. Ann and I were in our dressing-gowns, barefoot;

she looked wonderfully tousled, her features blurred with sleep,
her hair a tangle of browns and golds in the fireglow, naked under
her gown. She helped the boy with the wrapping paper. Soon,
the rug in front of the hearth was strewn with the crumpled paper,
itself a carpet of treasure, blues and silvers and purples and reds,
while the furniture held Harry's new toys, things of wood and
plastic, cheap, bright, noisy things which he put to his mouth to
lick and taste. Eventually he sat among the discarded wrappings
and began to play with them, tearing off the strips of sticky tape
and binding them into a ball. He ignored the toys in the fascination
of the coloured papers.

'So much for the presents,' I said. 'We could just have given
him a roll of Sellotape to play with, and a few old newspapers.'

'But that's what I've got for you,' laughed Ann. 'Here you
are . . .' And she knelt down to reach for a weighty parcel from
under the tree. On her knees at my feet, the front of her
dressing-gown falling open, she held out the gift to me with both
hands, bowed her head so that her hair tumbled over her face.
'For you,' she said.

I opened it slowly, taking care not to tear the golden paper. It
was a book, an expensive art book, alive with pages of glowing
Japanese painting. Every plate burned with colour. I turned
through it quickly: it was a forest fire of colours: figures at work
and at rest, the scenery of mountains and oceans, changing
seasons, fabulous creatures in their outlandish environments.

'Why, it's gorgeous, darling,' I whispered. 'What a splendid
present . . .'

'Wait a minute,' she said. 'There's a picture of you in there
somewhere. Page seventy-three, I think. Go on, have a look!'
Her hands were on my kneecaps, she leant forward and her eyes
tingled.

And there I was.

I was a man on a beach, a long empty beach which stretched
away and disappeared into a green haze in the distance. Apart
from the man, the shore was deserted. There was a turquoise
sky, boiling with clouds. The man was wearing a long red gown
which was tugged by the wind so that the shape of his lean body
was clearly defined. His face was not visible, for he was looking

out to sea. But the line he was holding went over the waves, and there was the cormorant, half-submerged, quite black among the green and white water: the thin neck with its little collar, the head tilted slightly upward, the beak just open and manhandling a silver fish.

'Archie,' I said. 'Well done, Archie, you've got one . . . now just let me haul you in. And there's me in my kimono, bloody freezing on the beach at Caernarfon. Marvellous, marvellous, thank you so much, Ann, my love. What a lovely, special present!'

I closed the book. But I was still that faceless figure on a windswept shore. My mind refused to give up the image, the scene remained so clearly that I felt a spasm of cold from the bitter wind go through my shoulders and chest. Ann put up her face. With my tongue I touched the opaque blue tips of her teeth. I heard my voice saying, 'I love you so much and I shall love you for ever,' but it was distant and muffled through the cotton wool of those boiling clouds.

Reaching into the pocket of my dressing-gown, I brought out my tiny parcel. I held it out to her. 'For you,' I said.

It was a treat to watch her. She was electric with pleasure, like a child. There was the fragile necklace and the butterfly nestling in the cotton wool of the box. She drew it out and it danced on the end of the chain like a living thing. Set against her throat, with her hair loose on the whiteness of her neck, it gleamed. Kneeling on the rug, her throat and shoulders and her breast bare, the reds of her hair, the marble flesh, the silken blue dressing-gown and the golden butterfly, she was a figure from the book of Japanese paintings, burning with colours and warmth, a smouldering woman. She kissed my knees and she kissed the palms of my hands. 'Thank you,' she whispered. 'I shall love you forever.'

The three of us had a bath. In the steam and enveloping heat of the bathroom, we manoeuvred into the tub, Ann and I at opposite ends with her legs draped over mine, and Harry squatting in the pool which was formed by our interlacing limbs. We poured cupfuls of water over his head, he splashed us with his sturdy fingers. He was agog at the closeness, the slipperiness of so much white flesh, falling against Ann and burying his face between her breasts, only to emerge and spit out the taste of soap. Then he explored the muscular worm which sprouted from the water between my legs, and he examined himself by way of comparison. The worm uncurled and held its head aloft, out of the soap-grey water. Ann decorated it with a thick lather. Harry was soaped from head to toe, a shining cherub. Ann knelt up and let the suds run down her body, so she glistened in a suit of white bubbles, while I slid my hands from her throat and over her breasts, whose nipples stood out abruptly, as big and as hard as acorns, down the smoothness of her belly and into the nest of soap-rich fur which sent its stream of lather onto her thighs. My hands stayed in the nest for a minute and moved about in there. She closed her eyes tightly and gripped the sides of the bath. Enmeshed between us, Harry wriggled in the grey water. He forced his hands into mine, into the stream of soap from Ann's thighs. And when I withdrew my fingers, it was little Harry, with a glassy grin frozen on his face, who continued to work the rich lather. Ann was oblivious. Her body tensed, her knuckles whitened as she gripped the bath, there was nothing she could do to stop the sudden rhythmic thrusts of her hips. She opened her eyes and mouth as wide as they would go. Harry looked up at his mother. She frowned at him as though he were a stranger whose name she ought to remember, said 'Bloody hell, bloody hell, oh bloody hell . . .' in a crescendo of whispers, before shuddering and subsiding into the water, her eyes once again tightly closed. A bubble of saliva formed at the corner of her mouth, as bright and as smooth as a pearl. Harry chuckled hoarsely and sprang to her breasts. She held him to her for a long moment, but when she opened her eyes she looked away from the little boy's sparkling face. He was a stranger to her, who had taken liberties she could not condone.

The water grew cooler. In front of the living-room fire, we dried each other and dressed.

The Knapps came in at midday. He looked fierce and flushed, a short man of forty made wiry by his daily running. His cheeks were unusually hollow, the gauntness emphasised by a closely cropped beard. Even that morning, he had completed his customary twelve miles, fighting against the clock over the tracks of the plantation, up and down the road to Beddgelert. While he ran each day and relaxed under the shower, his wife kept the post office and shop. She looked pretty in a flowery dress, her blond hair bobbed, her plumpness dressed with powder and perfumed for Christmas. I soon pressed a big glass of sherry into her hand. Mr Knapp wondered if there was any fruit juice, so I made up a drink with some of Harry's cordial. Ann hurried in from the kitchen, looking rather warm from her work with the Christmas dinner, to give a kiss to both the visitors and accept some sherry from me. She was wearing her special scarlet dress, quite revealing at the front and at the back, the golden butterfly quivering at her throat. We all relaxed in the armchairs before the fire, while dinner was cooking. Ann was in and out to check its progress. It was the first time that Mr Knapp had been inside our cottage, and I saw him puzzling over the crowded shelves of books and the modern prints. He did not speak much until I enquired about his running. He was a dour character, and I felt the unvoiced disapproval of my own lifestyle which was centred on the books, the typewriter, the living-room fire. It occurred to me to show him the cormorant and describe our successes on the shoreline, to enlarge on a side of my routine which took me well away from the hearth. I hesitated. Perhaps it was best to keep Archie in the background and enjoy a cosy Christmas Day.

Mrs Knapp disappeared into the kitchen with Ann, amid much giggling and refilling of glasses. Harry was quietly playing at the foot of the stairs, behind the sofa, there was just the occasional chuckle and sigh, the clatter of his new toys. He was well occupied. In the absence of any other conversation, I changed my mind and decided to introduce the other member of the family to our guest.

'You never met Archie, did you?'

The man frowned and looked around the room. 'Who?'

'Archie, our bird. I wondered if Ann had mentioned it to your wife in one of their afternoon chats. No?'

Mr Knapp's grizzled face remained blank.

'Well, come and have a look at this then.' I got up and put my glass on the mantelpiece. 'It's in the backyard. We'll have to go through the kitchen, if we can escape the clutches of the ladies.'

He followed me into the steam of the kitchen.

'Ann, can you keep an eye on Harry for a few minutes? He's playing quite happily by the stairs. I just want to show off our charming pet . . . Mr Knapp hasn't seen it yet.'

Ann's face was smudged with a frown, but then she shrugged and flicked me with her dishcloth. 'Go on, you silly men. Just leave us to do all the hard work . . .' And as we went out, she added, 'I hope you've left us some sherry. We don't slave away for nothing, you know.'

Mrs Knapp tinkled with laughter. She was already rather flushed, enjoying herself more than she thought she was going to. The sherry must have muted her memories of the cormorant, which Ann had described to her some weeks ago. If the bird was securely confined to its cage in the yard, she had no interest in it. And through the kitchen window, there had been no sight or sound of Archie since much earlier in the day.

We went into the garden, shivered at first at the touch of the cold after the warmth of the cottage. I had done nothing to keep it tidy since the onset of the wet weather in the autumn. Ferns and heathers trailed over the slates of the path, everything was bedraggled with the drenching of a grey morning. At the foot of the garden, the winter trees shone black. The stream boomed. The edges of the mist were tangled in the firs of the plantation on the hillside, the mountains themselves were lost in the cloud.

'Here we are. Come on, Archie, don't be shy. You've got a visitor.'

Inside the wire-mesh cage, the crate stood among the threads of straw. There was no movement or sound from the box. The cage and the silent crate were like an odd work of sculpture in some modern gallery, the box standing centre stage, the whiteness of the wood smeared with yellows and greens and browns. Mr Knapp had never been inside an art gallery, but his daily newspaper sometimes ridiculed the idiocies of abstract sculpture. He glanced at me, thinking perhaps that this was my idea of a joke, the sort of Christmas game which schoolteachers played. If so, it was as daft as those prints hanging on the living-room wall.

'Hey, Archie, it's Christmas Day. Don't be an unsociable bugger . . . come on, Scrooge!'

There was a rope which led from the box, through the wire, coiled up and then attached to the drainpipe by the kitchen window. The ladies moved like ghosts behind the steamed-up glass. I took the rope and pulled it tight, began to tug it gently, rocking the crate.

'Merry Christmas, Archie!' I called, and started to sing Good King Wenceslas, my voice oiled with sherry. The crate rocked more and more, there was no response. It swayed and toppled over. The cormorant fell out. It stood up and stretched, beating its wings and sending up the blades of straw, then stopped in mid-beat to adopt its more picturesque heraldic pose for the benefit of its new admirer. And Archie hissed.

'Hell's teeth . . .' whispered Mr Knapp, taking a step back-wards.

Hiding a smile behind my hand, I nodded my head in appreci-ation. 'A cormorant,' I said. '*Phalacrocorax carbo*, a second-year male, I think. We call it Archie. Quite a beast, eh? I've been fishing with it a few times from the beach at Caernarfon, caught bags of dabs and eels. I put a collar round its throat and a line to its ankle, wait until it's got something and then tug it in. Then you confiscate the fish and push the bird back out to sea. Make a lovely soup with the dabs and Archie eats all the eels. You should come with us next time we go: you'd be impressed.'

Mr Knapp was impressed. He was staring, open-mouthed, at the cormorant. Archie remained still, wings outspread, head erect, beak agape.

'Can be a bit temperamental,' I continued, 'a bit moody, you know what I mean? Not a goose, not a crow, not a gull . . . a cormorant, something of a sea-crow. In fact, the name's derived from the Latin, *corvus marinus*, which means exactly that. Great fisherman, with a disgraceful appetite: it'll eat almost anything.' I went to the wire. 'Come on, Archie. Don't be snooty, come and say hello.'

The bird folded its wings and waddled forward. It put its beak through the mesh. Moving my hands slowly, I touched the beak and stroked the glossy head. 'There's a good lad. I'll get you some tasty scraps when we've had our dinner. Haven't forgotten you, so there's no need for you to sulk in your box all day.'

The other man came to the cage.

'Always move really slowly,' I warned him, 'or it gets a bit jumpy. Seems pretty relaxed today though. Must be the Christmas spirit . . .'

Mr Knapp ran a finger along the cormorant's bill. I raised an eyebrow at the bird's patience with this stranger. The finger caressed the short feathers of Archie's throat. It closed its eyes.

'Well, well, you've made a conquest there,' I admitted. 'You're the first person, apart from me and its previous owner, who's had the honour of coming so close and actually touching the thing. Hope you're not getting soft, Archie.'

Just then, with the rattle of an opening window, there came Ann's voice: 'Come on, you two men, dinner's ready. We need some carving done . . .'

As though to prove it understood the words, the cormorant reacted. Archie withdrew the beak into the cage, away from the soporific movement of the finger, withdrew it with the same deliberate accumulation of tension as a man who pulls back the string of a longbow, and shot it forward again at the loosely dangling hand. The tip of the dagger-beak stabbed and raked, there was a sharp crack, like splintering wood. Mr Knapp leapt from the wire, bellowed a single obscenity and jammed the wounded hand under his armpit. Archie retreated into the furthest corner, shaking its head from the gloom. The man shouted a string of particularly unseasonal blasphemies at the cormorant. He exhaled a series of hisses from between whitened lips, looking as fierce as he often did at the end of a cross-country run, squeezing the hand under his arm and mouthing his favourite oath. I had watched the cormorant strike. Something told me that the beak was destined for the finger, just as Archie closed its eyelids and swooned in the luxury of the man's caresses. There was something so inevitable about it at that moment that I had been unable to speak a word of warning. So I simply watched.

We hurried into the kitchen.

'Your language, gentlemen . . .' began Ann, but I cut her off.

'Take a look at this hand, Ann, will you? That bugger Archie got him.'

She added her own choice of expletives to those of the injured man, glaring first at me and then out of the window, at the cage. Mrs Knapp went very pale, but she managed to extricate the hand from her husband's armpit. Harry came to the kitchen, on hearing the commotion. He stood at the door, smiling like an angel. Among the numerous pots and pans which were empty and awaiting washing, with steam rising from three dishes of vegetables, different sauces and gravy, with the golden carcass of the turkey crackling gently to itself in a bath of its own juices, somehow a space was cleared so that the wound could be attended to. The man hopped from foot to foot at the touch of cold water, hissing like a kettle. His wife washed and dried the hand, dabbed some disinfectant on the broken skin. At this, Mr Knapp yelped, and Harry chuckled so loudly that I felt it was tactful to shoo him back into the living-room. In fact, the extent of the cut was not severe: it seemed that the beak had struck a hammer blow rather than a stab: there was the first flowering of a big bruise and the suspicion that the little finger was fractured. His hand was bandaged. He accepted a glass of sherry to replace his customary orange juice. The colour returned to his thin cheeks. Ann and I could not apologise enough; she gave her guests another kiss each and sat them down at the dining-table we had set up in front of the fire. Returning to the kitchen to collect the vegetables and the meat I was carving, she wheeled on me, her eyes ablaze.

'For heaven's sake, what do you think you were doing out there? You let him touch that crazy bird? The thing's a killer!'

'It seemed to be all right today. He stroked it, so it closed its eyes and let him carry on. You startled it by calling out of the window . . .'

'Oh, charming!' she exclaimed. 'Was it my fault then? Did I frighten your darling bird? The poor sensitive little thing . . .'

'Of course it wasn't your fault, love. I didn't mean to sound like that. It all just happened in a flash. It needn't spoil our day, he'll be OK, he's got a broken finger, that's all. He's a tough guy, he'll tell everyone who goes into the shop and love every minute of it.' I kissed her cheek. 'I'll carve, you take everything through to the patient and his wife.'

She shrugged, forced a wry smile. 'This is madness. You know, not one of my friends in the suburbs of Derby has got a bloody cormorant in the backyard. The poor deprived souls, they don't know what delights they're missing . . .' Still muttering to herself, she went into the living-room with two dishes of vegetables.

It was a delicious meal. Ann had excelled herself. She pointed out that it was her wonderful husband who had done all the shopping, making the arduous journey into Caernarfon several times, with no thought for his own entertainment. I responded by reaching under the cloth in the pretence of retrieving my fallen napkin, to run my hand along the inside of her thigh.

She was a little red-faced when I emerged again with the napkin. There was plenty of wine. Mr Knapp declared a lifting of his personal ban on the drinking of alcohol, brandishing the wounded hand. The blood was seeping through the bandage and had stained the table-cloth as well. He wore it like a badge. 'Don't fuss, dear,' he said, waving away the attentions of his wife. 'Bit of blood and a broken finger, that's all. I'll be pounding those roads again tomorrow morning, you'll see . . .'

Harry was subdued. He ate what Ann gave him, but kept his eyes on the man and his growing blossom of blood.

The courses came and went with the opening and emptying of more bottles of wine. I got up to fuel the fire, Ann was back and forth to the kitchen, Harry watched us all from within his private world of silence. He flinched at the pop of the corks, and he smiled to see me throw each cork among the flames, signalling our intention of finishing a bottle once it was started. The child seemed to be studying us all, from a great distance, almost as though he were a towering adult intent on the stirring of an ant-hill. Once or twice, his eyes flickered from the bloodstained bandage to meet my eyes, and he would smile a lazy smile, as if we were sharing a private joke. Just as Ann had said before: he was like an adult, withdrawn and somewhat vacant, content to watch us and smile knowingly to himself.

It was the longest and most leisurely meal that we had had in the cottage. More wine, a drop more brandy, then the coffee pot lingered on the table and was replenished in the kitchen. Harry was encouraged to leave the table. He continued his exploration of the breaking points of his new toys; only a few gurgling cries were heard from behind the sofa, and his little blond head appeared now and then to remind us that he was still there and aware of every gesture we made. The Queen's speech began on the radio. We four adults sat in silence and listened, the Knapps with sombre faces, while I walked my errant hand along Ann's thigh. She pushed me away with one of her fierce teacher's glares, but locked her fingers into mine. 'Amen,' I said, as soon as the speech was finished, and quickly turned off the radio before the anthem started, to avoid the possibility of the Knapps' jumping to their feet.

Outside, the light was already fading on a grey afternoon. There was no traffic. The village was as silent as the mountains. As soon as the debris was cleared into the kitchen and Ann had firmly refused all offers of help with the washing-up, we sank back into our armchairs. I put two logs on the fire. For a minute, the flames were muted. Then the golden tongues licked round the dry wood and the room was splashed with their glow. The lights of the Christmas tree shone. On the carpet were the scarlet and purple ribbons of discarded wrapping paper, the litter of pine needles, the wine bottles which twinkled in the growing blaze, the confusion of Harry's toys. The room was warm and full of colour. Ann looked as though she would begin to purr loudly at any moment, curled up in her armchair, the red dress and its glimpses of her breasts. Mr Knapp put his head back; he seemed to have forgotten the throb in his hand in the fullness of food and wine. His wife was already asleep. Silence, save for the occasional spitting of the logs. My eyelids were heavy, becoming heavier, my head swam a little when I closed my eyes. Silence, and the inviting oblivion of sleep . . .

Only Harry remained wide awake.

He came round from his toys behind the sofa, stood on the rug in front of the fire. He looked at the four adults, one after the other. The fierce-looking stranger was asleep, making a whistling noise through his beard. The lady was asleep too. His mother was asleep. Harry looked at me. I watched him through flickering eyelids. Again our eyes met, and he smiled his grown-up smile. He turned to the tree, took a handful of the needles and put them in his mouth. Then he blew them onto the carpet. It was lovely, close to the fire. For a while, he just looked into its magic places, all the different shapes and colours, faces, animals, birds. He put his cheeks nearer to the flames, withdrew them at the blast of heat. There was such a groaning inevitability about the way he turned from his study of the fire to look again at me, such deliberation in his straightening up and his reappraisal of the slumbering adults, that I felt myself weighted down, sucked irresistibly into the softness of my armchair. And, just as I had known of the cormorant's intention even before it withdrew its beak from the stranger's caresses, as I had watched it strike and been unable to speak, again I was frozen into inaction by the shape of the smile on Harry's face. There was nothing I could do. I simply watched him from my armchair. His smile showed that he knew I would do nothing to stop him. The room was quiet, the house was silent. Only the regular breathing of the sleepers, a fall of embers from the fire. Harry stood on the hearth-rug. He was listening. His little body quivered in the strain of listening. He sniffed the air. He sniffed again, more than anything else in the world like a rat in a sewer, the nostrils twitching, the lips a-tremble.

With a final dismissive glance in my direction, he stepped over the splayed-out legs of the sleepers and went to the living-room door. He opened it, standing on tip-toe and stretching up to the handle. I heard him go into the kitchen.

I closed my eyes. I knew what Harry was doing.

In the kitchen, he halted. Completely still. Listening, listening. Sniffing the air. He walked the few steps to the back door. Stretched up. Opened it.

Harry stepped into the backyard. It was dark and very cold. Everything was still. He waited in the utter stillness.

Something was moving in the darkness.

A black thing was moving among the enveloping blackness of the yard. The thing creaked and hissed. Harry looked and listened and sniffed, went towards it, deeper into the dark.

He was lost in the shadows.

*   *   *

Someone was shaking me. It was Ann.

'Come on, sleepy head,' she said, tugging my elbow. 'Come on, rouse yourself.'

I sat up and leaned forward. It was cold, there was a fearful draught from somewhere. Five o'clock. The fire had burned right down, the room was gloomy. My tongue felt woolly, too big for my mouth. I had a thick head.

'Oh dear,' I said very quietly. I said it again, rubbing my forehead.

Mr Knapp awoke with a start and stared around the dark room, as though for a moment he could not remember where he was. His wife was the last to emerge from sleep, as slow as a beached porpoise.

'Stoke up the fire,' said Ann. 'I think some good strong tea is needed.'

She got up and went to the door.

'Are you there, Harry?' she called out vaguely, expecting an answering cry from behind the sofa or from near the tree. Shutting the door and shuddering at the chill which was coming through from the kitchen, she turned back towards the fire.

'Poor little Harry, have we been ignoring you on Christmas Day? It's naughty Daddy's fault, with all his brandy . . .' She cuffed me on the shoulder. 'You naughty man, sending us all off to sleep.'

She sat down again.

'Harry? Come on, Harry, are you there?'

Then she sprang to her feet. In a second, she reached the switch and put on the light. Mr Knapp groaned and covered his eyes. Ann was through the room like a panther, behind every piece of furniture, glancing under the tree.

'Oh Christ . . .' and she went up the stairs three at a time. Then she was down again. 'Oh Christ, the door . . . he's gone out!'

I was on my feet, quite unsteady, listening to the rumbling of surf inside my head. But I was right behind Ann as she burst into the kitchen. She turned on the light, gasped at the sight of the open door. The room was bitterly cold.

'Go on . . . go and look!' She was transfixed, urging me past her. 'Please, go and look! I'm . . .'

She was quivering. The muscles in her face were all moving, her hands fluttered like terns at the corners of her mouth. Before I could galvanise myself, dispel the cobwebs of sleep from around my eyes, she began to sob, her face twisted with fear, tumbling tears through every line in her cheeks.

I went out. The light from the kitchen lit the yard and some parts of the garden. With a quick look at the cormorant, which was standing quite still by its crate, I dashed past the cage and down to the stream. I bellowed at the torrent of black water. 'Harry! Harry! Are you there, Harry?'

There was Ann's voice at the door, cracked with bewilderment and horror. 'Find him, find him! Is he there? Oh, find him, please, please . . .'

The Knapps were in the kitchen, peering through the window. I came back up the garden, halted and searched through every bush and brake of bracken, kicking aside the tangles of fuchsia. I must have been sleeping still. There was a whistling in my ears. Ann was there too. She tore out great clumps of honeysuckle which had grown over the fence and onto the ground. She was crying very loudly. Mr Knapp ran past us to the stream. I nearly shouted out to him, to stop him, but my mouth formed the words and there was no sound. He went splashing into the water, pushing aside the overhanging branches of the trees. Through her sobs, Ann was yelling, 'Come on, Harry! Where are you, Harry? Oh fucking Christmas . . .'

Dripping wet from his thighs downwards, Mr Knapp came up to the light again.

'Can't see anything by the stream. Got a torch?' He shouted to his wife. 'Run and get that torch from the shop! Run, woman!' But before she could move, there came a commotion from the cormorant's cage. Whereas Archie had been standing still, seemingly dazzled by the sudden glare from the kitchen and confused by the shouting, now it clapped its wings and launched itself at the wire. Hissing like a nest of vipers, it forced its head through the mesh, scrabbled on the wire with its black feet. Mr Knapp shook his bandaged fist at it. 'And you can stay away from me!'

he stormed. Turning back to his wife, 'Get the torch, what's the matter with you, woman?'

And I intervened. I had been staring at the bird, at the cage.

'No,' I said. 'Wait. We don't need a torch.'

The cage door was open. The section of mesh, which I could remove and replace when taking Archie out of the cage or putting it back in again, was loose. Ann was holding her breath. I went into the cage. The cormorant retreated from the wire and stood by its crate, the white box which was still on its side since the bird's rude awakening that morning, stuffed with straw. Archie bristled and came forward, head held low, the beak brandished like a razor in the hand of a drunk. This time there was no retreat: the bird shot at my ankles with the speed of a snake, and the beak cracked on my shin. In a second, it was by the crate again. The cormorant spread its wings across the tumble of straw.

'Bugger!'

I rubbed the shin vigorously with both hands. There was blood on my trousers and sock. Archie waited, spreadeagled in front of the crate, ready to defend its territory.

Ann moved closer to the wire mesh, from where she could see behind the cormorant to the overturned box and the threads of straw which had fallen from it. As I advanced again and the bird angled down its writhing neck to aim low and avoid my grabbing hands, she saw into the thick bedding of the crate. There was Harry, snug and warm in the cormorant's nest. The little blond head stirred in the straw. His face looked out, calm and serious.

'Harry, Harry! Come out of there! Come to mummy!' The tears fell faster.

Mr Knapp was shouting. 'The kid's in the bloody crate!' He ran into the cage behind me, ducking through the loose section. 'I'll sort out the bloody bird . . . you get the boy!'

Pushing me to one side, he raged towards the cormorant. It flailed the beak and caught the dangling end of the bandage, flapped backwards into the corner with the unravelling red and white strip. With an incoherent bellow of anger, he bore down on the bird. He hopped forward and held up the other foot as his only weapon. Twice, three times the beak struck the thick rubber sole, bounced off. There was a length of bandage from his hand to the bird, wound

around his outstretched leg and around the cormorant's neck, like
a bizarre Christmas decoration, a ribbon of white splashed with red.
Keeping Archie at bay in the corner, he yelled over his shoulder,
'Get the crate! Harry's in the crate!' But I could only move slowly,
as though my limbs were weighted down. My mind was nearly
stopped, something pressed on me and made everything slow. The
voices in my head were deep and distorted, as incomprehensible
as the voice on a tape recorder which is playing too slowly. Somewhere, someone's finger was pressing on the record, making the
voices grind and limp. There was no sense in them. In the crate?
Why should Harry be in Archie's crate? What did this man mean: in
the crate? I felt a shove in my back and moved forward. There was
Ann by my side. Her face was very close to mine, her mouth was
moving, opening and closing, she was shouting but I couldn't hear
. . . only the rumble of voices, as though I were underwater and
the only sound was the thunder of waves breaking overhead. I
watched my own hands as they gripped the edges of the crate, I
was a spectator, the hands lifted the box upright, there were my
wife's hands too, next to mine, they were half lifting and half dragging the crate out of the cage. Still the crashing of surf, the grumble
of underwater voices. Outside the cage . . . the man was hopping
to the door, with the black cormorant stuck like a leech to his
leg, some filthy bloodsucking bat fixed on his flesh, leather wings,
leathery feet, an unblinking eye, that beak . . . outside the cage. I
found I was surfacing, it was lighter, my head cleared the surf . . .

Ann was moaning. 'Harry, Harry, Harry, my little Harry . . .'
She had lifted him out of the straw-filled box. She stroked his
blond hair and picked off the threads of straw which stuck to his
clothes. Then her hand wiped her own eyes, dabbed at her streaming nostrils. 'Let's have you inside.' She went in, with Mrs Knapp.

Mr Knapp was fixing the door of the cage.

'The crate,' I said weakly, 'what about its crate? Archie will be
cold tonight if it hasn't got its crate in the cage . . .'

The man stared at me, muttered something which I couldn't
hear, and bent to examine his torn and blood-stained trousers.
There was blood on his hand again. The bandage was in the cage,
draped like a scarf around the cormorant's neck.

'Look at your leg,' said Mr Knapp. 'Let's go in.'

And so to the living-room for an examination of wounds. The two women were unhurt. Mrs Knapp was numb with the inability to understand and feel. She sat before the fire, quite numb. All those cries, and the swearing, her husband soaked to the skin and streaked with blood; the child lying still in a white wooden crate. And that desperate bird. It was like one of those daft plays she sometimes watched on television, a lot of swearing, and women crying. Ann was quivering still, with anger and shock. Her eyes were swollen. She washed her face in the bathroom and combed her hair. But she looked as though she would explode again at any time into another torrent of tears, as though she would have to stand up and pace the room to ventilate her pent-up rage. Lying back in the armchair, with Harry sitting still on her lap, she took a series of deep breaths which set the butterfly dancing on her throat. There had been the awful splashing of Mr Knapp in the black water of the stream, the calmness of Harry's face as he looked at her out of the straw of the cormorant's crate: the idea of the child walking through the kitchen, into the yard, to unfasten the door of the cage and step inside . . . to clamber into the box and snuggle down among that stinking straw. She roused herself and shook the boy. 'Why, Harry? Why, why, why?' But her hissing questions were ignored. Harry stared at her and blinked very slowly, like a lizard.

Mr Knapp dressed his wounds. His wife watched him, speechless. He rolled up his wet trousers above the knee. There were four or five gashes on one leg, the leg he had proffered as a target for the cormorant, none of them very deep: holding his foot up to the bird, he had deflected the blows with his shoe. He dabbed them with disinfectant. A fresh bandage was put around his hand, once the bleeding was staunched. Since midday, his broken finger had turned blue. Once the holiday was over, it would need the attention of a doctor. The single jab which Archie had delivered to my shin was the most severe wound of the evening. It had struck where the flesh was thinnest, right on the bone. My trousers and my sock and shoe were covered with blood. I started to clean the opening, but when I saw that the bone was exposed under a loose flap of skin, I shivered and stopped. I just laid the skin back again, closed my eyes. It hurt.

Harry seemed unaffected. Once Ann had swept him off to the bathroom to sponge away the smell of the straw and the pungent slime of the cormorant, the little boy seemed to shed the uncanny vigilance of the inquisitive rodent and become a child again. He sat down on the hearth-rug, sweet-smelling in his bright pyjamas, and busied himself with his toys. There was firelight in his hair, the shadows of the flames on his cheeks. He looked up at us, four bewildered adults, and smiled an innocent smile. There was nothing on his face or in his manner which recalled his union with Archie. Only, the golden power of the fire seemed to envelop him.

The Knapps stood up and suggested that they should go. They had had an enjoyable and eventful Christmas Day, a lovely meal, perhaps a little too much to drink in the afternoon: something of a fright that evening, but fortunately no real harm had been done. She buttoned up her coat and made her speech of thanks while her husband waited in silence. He looked faintly ridiculous, his trousers wet, the clumsy bandage leaking again, and his expression of ferocious bafflement. With a nod, Ann took Mrs Knapp into the kitchen, holding Harry to her breast. I rose stiffly from my armchair.

'I'm very sorry about your hand,' I said, 'and about all that panic this evening. I'm glad you were here though. Thank you for your help.'

I was going to repeat my earlier invitation to the fishing expeditions, but hesitated, deciding that it might not be the appropriate moment. Maybe when the finger was mended.

'Don't mention it,' replied the wounded man. 'I don't envy you having that thing in the backyard, I must admit. Bloody poisonous, in my opinion. Amazing that it didn't go for the boy, when you stop to think about it. Lucky lad, your Harry.' He added, 'Get that leg sorted out quickly. It needs a good clean, for a start.'

The women came back into the living-room. I could tell from Ann's expression, the pinched brow, that they had had a short but conclusive woman's talk. Mrs Knapp made a little sign to her husband, to which he responded with a similar twitch of the head. Such are the codes perfected between husband and wife. She spoke directly to me.

'Ann's decided to come over the road and stay with us tonight, with Harry, of course.' The woman cleared her throat. 'I don't know whether you're at all interested in my opinion, but there it is anyway. I think you should get rid of that bird as soon as possible. If you didn't have a baby boy,' and she raised her eyebrows in a gesture towards Harry, who was staring owlishly at her from his mother's arms, 'then it might be different. But it's just not . . .' Her speech dried up. After a deep breath, she continued. 'So Ann and Harry are coming over the road with us tonight. Give you time to get that bird sorted out, or something.' To her husband, 'All right, dear? We've got the spare room. It's all ready.'

I began to speak. 'Look, Ann, what's the . . . ?'

But she silenced me with her outburst and the flaring of colour in her cheeks. Her eyes crackled.

'No! I'm frightened! I'm going to be sick if I stay anywhere near that thing any longer . . .' She was barely able to control the shaking of her voice. 'Please, love, I can't talk about it. I'm going to . . .'

And she ran upstairs with Harry.

'So whose bloody idea was this? Eh? What's all this whispering in the kitchen? Eh? Come on, Mrs bloody Knapp, who suggested it?'

'Calm down, my lad,' interrupted her husband. 'No need to use that tone. We're all shocked, my wife as well.'

'Oh Christ!' I shouted, turning to the stairs just as Ann came down. She and Harry had their coats on. She was carrying the boy with one arm and a small case in the other.

'What the hell's the matter with you?' I was saying. 'The boy's all right, isn't he? Not a scratch on him! So where do you think you're going?'

She pushed past me to the front door.

'Please can we go now?' she said to the Knapps. They went out. Ann turned back to me. 'Can't you see anything? Haven't you seen anything? Think about it, my love, think about it all. Not just what happened this evening. I'm frightened. I don't understand it . . .'

She kissed me quickly and stepped to the door. It closed. I heard her footsteps on the pavement, over the road, the key in the front door of the Knapps' house, their door opening, shutting.

Silence.

I was left alone in a silent house, with the lingering image of Harry's face over Ann's shoulder as they went out: the face of a cherub, scarred with a manic grin.

Christmas Day. Six o'clock in the evening.

Outside, darkness and the start of another soaking of fine drizzle. Dirty snow.

Inside, a room full of all the gew-gaws of a Christmas at home: the fire, the tree, the toys, the sherry, the decorations. But all spoiled by two incongruous elements: the absence of people, the pervasive stink of antiseptic.

I turned off the main light of the room and put another log on the fire. I turned off the lights of the Christmas tree. Filling my glass with sherry, I sat down on the rug and waited for the flames to flicker around the dry wood. I wondered for a moment whether I was going to cry. I did not.

Presently, the fresh log was ablaze. Three times I refilled my glass. In the firelight, I examined again my wounded shin. The blood on my trousers was dry, the fabric lined with a black crust. Blood was still oozing from the gash. My sock and shoe were sticky. The flap of skin was stuck down in the congealing scab. I knew that the silver glimmer of bone lay just beneath. It had stopped hurting. Quite soon I would have the courage and the will to clean the wound and anoint it with the stinging disinfectant, after another drink perhaps. More sherry, less pain. What a brilliant discovery, I thought. It made me smile. So I could still make something of the remaining hours. Bugger the tree, the hysterical wife and her bloody inquisitive child, bugger the Knapps, bugger that bird. Another glass of sherry. Pulling up my trouser leg again, I poured a few drops onto the scab. It stung, but I heard myself laugh with a braying sort of laugh as I rolled backwards to lie on the hearth-rug. Why did the sherry work as an anaesthetic at one end and sting like a scorpion at the other? It was magic, the kind of magic I didn't want to understand. Some Philistine like bloody Mr Knapp would know the answer, or my clever very sensitive wife. The women thought they knew everything: they had their whispered debates in the kitchen, like a coven of witches, only to emerge as coherent as a school of bottle-nosed dolphins. And there was Mrs Knapp suddenly taking charge, calm and efficient like a staff nurse from one of her mid-morning soap operas. My voice sang out in an imitation of her ludicrous advice: 'I think you should get rid . . .' A toast was in order, this Christmas Day. I raised my glass to the flames and admired the jewels of light which sparkled from the sherry. Better stand up, do it properly, but I staggered before the hearth, unsteady on my feet. And there, with blood on my hands from the exploration of my wound, I proposed the toast.

'Ladies and gentlemen, members of the jury: be upstanding. To Ann, my supersensitive wife, much cleverer and more sensitive than I could ever be. To Harry, who can't keep his pestering fingers to himself. To the bloody Knapps, one of them pounding the endless trails of the forest, the other stranded like a mermaid washed up in front of the telly. And, of course, to Archie, the mighty hunter, the vampire bat, the sea-crow, *phalacrocorax carbo* . . . Ladies and gentlemen, a toast: may they all be undone. God save the Queen.'

Draining my glass, I toppled back on the rug. Again, as I looked into the flames of the fire, I wondered whether I was going to cry. Not quite. Not yet.

The bottle was empty. The last drop clung for a second to the rim, before falling onto the oozing shin. This time, it did not sting. I got up by pulling myself onto the arm of the sofa, sat there until I was confident that I could negotiate the next stage of the operation, stood up abruptly and went to the front door. I took my coat from the peg and put it on. There was my wallet in the pocket, and a box of matches. That was all I needed. Why should I sit in the cottage on Christmas evening, with nothing to look at but the embers of the fire, nothing to talk to but the collective spectre of my old staffroom, nothing left to drink? I would celebrate. There remained a few hours of Christmas Day.

Between the cottage and the pub, I walked slowly and sucked in the cool air. It was drizzling, nothing more. Glancing up at the windows of the Knapps' house as I went by, I saw the movement of figures behind the curtains, the flicker of a fire or, more likely, their television. I snorted, turned up my collar and walked on. Outside the pub, the road was lined with cars. Shouts and laughter drifted to me and past me, vanishing in the light rain which speckled my glasses. Snowdon was invisible. The stream grumbled under the bridge, came out on the other side of the road with the whoosh of an express train. Much too rough for Archie. But I would bring Harry one afternoon and show him the foaming torrent. He'd like it. I looked through the windows of the pub before going in. It was crowded, I would have to wrestle my way to the bar, through the smiles and the smoke and the season's greetings. Mercifully, the Christmas carols were muffled by the noise. When I opened the door, a wave of sound broke over my head.

Somehow I found my way to the bar. I had the impression that, rather than having to elbow and jostle through the barrier of people, they moved aside, I seemed to cleave them apart and there I was, leaning on the soggy beer mats, looking down at a number of filthy ashtrays and beer glasses. The eyes of the drinkers who were sitting in the lounge were drawn to me, sucked along by the draught of cold air which followed me from the door. My coat was damp with drizzle, my spectacles immediately steamed up. The eyes arrived at my blood-stained trousers. Someone was pointing, I heard the whispers: 'Jesus, look at his foot as well . . . Does he know? . . . Leave him alone, of course he knows . . .' My drink stood on the bar, I paid for it and drank half the pint in a couple of gulps. Then I belched loudly, tried hard for half a minute to summon a fart by clenching the buttocks and the stomach muscles: nothing. Meanwhile, I drained the rest of the beer and ordered another. Quite a successful belch just then, deep and resounding, a belch that Harry Belafonte would have been proud of. I contrived to display the gory foot to its best advantage. Bending down, I hitched up the trouser leg to the knee and had the satisfaction of hearing one or two gasps from the onlookers. The bleeding had stopped. The entire shin was caked in blood. I dropped the trouser leg and returned to my drink. My industry was rewarded with the fart, only a squeak, but enough to attract the sneers of a pretty girl who was standing nearby. The beer was slipping down well. Business at the bar was furious, I was trapped there by an everchanging wall of customers. There were faces very close to mine, they grinned and breathed within a few inches of me. Some of these people spoke to me, wishing me a Happy Christmas, but my tongue refused to respond so I simply nodded. I heard somebody mention Ann, and Harry's name was whispered. For a while, I thought I could hear myself speaking, but it was like listening to a poor recording of my own voice, it seemed distant, disembodied, as one's voice sounds different through the machinery of a tape recorder. I watched a hand move slowly towards my glass and lift it up, realised it was my own hand, and the glass came closer to my lips. The girl behind the bar, very attractive but terminally Welsh, refilled the glass and helped herself to money from my wallet. It was suddenly noisier, there was a rush of noise as though one of those bloody jets was hurtling overhead, then it faded away. Laughter and shouts, the clattering of glasses, some singing, the muted tinkle of the carols, the pinging of the till: the sounds came and went, gently and regularly, like surf on a shingle shore. Someone knocked against the shin, I heard a voice, the voice from the tape recorder, say 'Bugger . . .' quite loudly, and there was a stab of pain. And then all the voices in the bar joined in a crashing wave. The hand brought the glass once more to my mouth, and I demolished another pint. Before I could extricate my wallet from my pocket, the replacement was foaming in front of me, and this time the barmaid waved away my money with a gesture towards the crowd. I turned slowly, shifting my stiffening leg carefully among the feet of the other revellers, and I nodded vaguely in the direction the girl had indicated. But it was impossible to make out and recognise the individual faces: there was only a cloud of smoke which drifted around the heads and shoulders of a babbling throng. Facing the bar, I found that the crowd had squeezed even closer, so that my essential prop, the spot where my elbow had been wedged for support, was out of reach. I could only just wriggle my hand through to fetch my pint. The loss of blood was affecting me more, the rushing in my ears unsteadied me a bit and I gripped a nearby arm, a strong one fortunately, for it held me up although I lost a quarter of my drink. Forcing my way back to the bar, I lodged myself against a wooden pillar. That was better: security of tenure, and the sweet scent of a girl's neck a few inches from my face. And there was my glass, miraculously full to the brim once more, the barmaid signalling into the crowd. Jesus, this was a feast . . . and I waved an arm to show my appreciation of the benefactor. The pall of smoke billowed to the ceiling, trickles of smoke from so many lips and mouths, a surging mass of faces in front of me, all of them grey and wreathed with smoke. But somewhere among them, a generous soul, the anonymous donor of my Christmas beer. I waved again. I heard my voice, muffled with smoke, and turned to the safety of the bar. It was noisy, everything heaved around me, the girl's neck drew close and then receded, my glass was weaving about in front of my lips, it was so bloody hot too . . . I drank most of the beer in one long draught: once the glass was fixed to my mouth it seemed sensible to keep it there instead of going to all the trouble of retracing the route to the bar and to the lips again with all the twists and turns of one of those heat-seeking missiles . . . then the hand released the glass, I heard it smash on the floor. For a second, I had the clear impression of the girl's neck rushing towards my face and striking me hard on the bridge of the nose, and I was toppled from the bar among a jungle of legs and feet and the shards of my beer glass. Shouting, a lot of shouting. But essentially it was quieter and cooler down there, as though I had ducked my head below the crashing surf to a less chaotic world. I would have stayed there longer, except that some meddling do-gooders were lifting me and manhandling me towards the door. A delicious taste of fresh air . . . my head reeled and there was a splendid fireworks display for a moment . . . and I was sitting outside the pub on a damp wooden bench.

I don't know how long I sat there in the drizzle. But the air was a tonic, after its first assault. I drank it in as gratefully as I had drunk the sherry and the beer. Only a few hundred yards from the front door of the cottage, but I didn't think I could safely negotiate the distance. When I tried to stand, it was as though the ground beneath my feet began to move on rollers, a fiendish kind of escalator or conveyor-belt which I couldn't keep pace with. So I sat down again and tried to focus my eyes on some distant object, the number plate of a parked car, concentrated on reading it until it swam away. In any case, what was the great hurry to get home? There was no-one there, no Ann, no Harry.

And at this, I felt a sudden rush of unhappiness, as traumatic and debilitating as a punch in the stomach. It brought the immediate stinging of tears. At last, I thought, now you can do it, now you can cry. Christmas fucking Day, so pissed that you can't even get to your own front door, with blood on your socks, a shin cut to the bone and probably wriggling with the nameless maggots that cormorants pick out of their feathers, abandoned by your wife and son . . . The tears came, thick and hot. I tasted the salt in the corners of my mouth and the running of my nose. The only handkerchief I could muster from my pocket was covered with dried blood. I threw it into the puddles with a snort of disgust and wiped my nose on the sleeve of my coat. Like a bloody vagrant. A roadside vagrant, overwhelmed by tears.

Behind me the door opened and closed. I sat upright and turned away my face, ashamed of the tears. Even that sudden movement brought a wave of nausea. To control it, I stared hard at another number plate, forced it into focus with a mighty effort of squinting, read it aloud, shut my eyes and recited the sequence two or three times. I looked again and checked that I had learned it by heart. People scuttled past me to the shelter of their cars. Lights came on, engines started, off they went with their tyres hissing on the wet road. I stopped crying. When I glanced along the street into the village, I saw that all the lights in the Knapps' house were off. In the aftermath of sorrow and self-pity, anger against the cormorant began to grow. If only I could mobilise myself and get to the cottage, I would sort it out once and for all. Archie must go, Ann and Harry were more important. I would wring its neck and toss the corpse into the stream, let it hurtle downstream to its beloved estuary along with so much other household rubbish. We'd abandon the cottage and go back to the suburbs of Derby . . . oh Christ, the numbing chores of school, the suburban semi, the television, the lawnmower, Saturday sodding football on the park . . .

Again there was movement around me as people began to leave the pub.

'All right, son?' from one enquiring voice.

'That leg's a mess,' from a woman this time.

'Oh that?' It was my own voice, thick with drink. 'That was when

I was attacked by my pet cormorant, *phalacrocorax carbo* . . .'

There was somebody standing next to me, not speaking. When the others had gone and the sounds of their car had faded away, the figure remained. I sniffed and averted my tear-stained face. I didn't want any well-meaning banter or, even worse, the commiserations of another maudlin drunk. I got to my feet and clutched the back of the bench. The conveyor-belt started, I had to lurch forward a few steps to stay on it. There seemed to be a hand at my elbow, very strong so that I instinctively leaned on it and felt its support. The escalator surged and I accelerated to keep up, comfortably aware of the strength beside me. Once in motion, practically upright, it was best to carry on.

'Only just along the street,' I heard myself saying. 'Little cottage on the right, nearly there now.'

I stepped out, swayed violently towards the road. The hand buoyed me up, restraining me from falling over the kerb. Looking down at the pavement, I watched the slabs go racing along under my feet, so fast that I felt nothing, like walking on cotton wool. One bloody foot and the bloody mess of my trousers, the other shoe clean, especially clean for Christmas Day. And through the blur of my bewhiskered vision, the heavy shoes of my Samaritan, very sensible and sturdy, the polished toe-caps poppled with raindrops. The pavement swooped up at me, I touched it with my fingers, could feel its wetness. A close-up of the big shoes and then again I was heaved to the vertical.

'This is it . . .'

But the door was already pushed open. Lights flicked on. I was dropped into an armchair, lying back with my eyes closed.

'Oh Christ . . .'

I had to sit up very quickly as the blackness behind my eyelids began to spin, erupting in different colours. With my head in my hands, I peered between my fingers at the living-room carpet. Somebody was putting another log onto the embers of the fire, turning on the lights of the Christmas tree. My head swam, everything was a blur of blue smoke. The footsteps went into the kitchen. Dimly, through the maelstrom of confused sounds which howled inside my mind, I heard the shooting of the bolt on the back door. Immediately there was a bitter draught through the room, the curtains whispered. But the footsteps returned, the draught remained, I felt a hand on my head for a tiny second, gentle as the landing of an autumn leaf. I heard the heavy shoes go to the front door and finally go out. The door closed. There was silence.

It was much too late for anyone to hear my blurted cry of gratitude. Minutes passed after the closing of the door. But I remembered to call out, I heard my own voice.

'Thank you, Uncle Ian. Thank you . . .'

This time, when I closed my eyes, the blackness was steady. So I slept.

When I woke up, the fire had gone out and the room was cold. It was nearly three o'clock in the morning. The main light and the lights of the Christmas tree were on: the sudden brightness hurt my eyes. I sat up in the armchair. There was a throbbing pain in my shin, it was pulsing hotly, and my head was singing. What I needed was to fetch a couple of blankets from upstairs and bed down again on the sofa with all the lights off: the swiftest return to oblivion. I had been woken, however, by my thirst and the urgent desire to piss. Standing up, with my hands over my forehead against the glare of the light, I found, not surprisingly, that I was still very drunk. The movement brought a rushing sound in my ears as though a dam had burst within my skull, the pulse in my legs speeded up, but I seemed a little steadier on my feet. I could remember a few things about the previous evening: drinking at the bar, sitting outside in the drizzle, a fractured image of the journey home. When I was sober again, I might try to piece it all together. Meanwhile, if I didn't get to the bathroom quickly, I was going to wet myself. Taking a deep breath, I turned to the door.

Archie was perched on the back of my armchair.

I peered at the cormorant through my fingers. It was sleeping, its wings folded, its face and beak buried in the feathers of its breast: a piece of modern sculpture, not out of place in the room with its prints and books and rugs, a green-black angular study of the bird asleep, forged from steel and burnt to its dark colours, twisted metal, twisted and scorched to make this effigy of the cormorant. The feet were folded over the back of the chair and the tail was a prop. Archie looked vulnerable in its sleep: not a hunter or a stabber or an arrogant squirter of shit. Simply a bird, lost in dreams.

I waited, completely still, lest the cormorant should wake. The door to the kitchen was open, and the draught which came into the living-room told me that the back door into the yard was wide open too. Footsteps . . . I remembered the footsteps, someone moving in the room while I lay inert in my drunkenness. But why? What was I supposed to do next? My drunkenness swept over me again. It was all too complicated. Who had arranged all this? And who assumed that I would merely play my part? It made me angry. I was cold, my head hurt, my mouth was full of cobwebs, the leg was squirming with worms . . . and there, calmly perched on the living-room furniture as though it were a household pet, was the vile Archie which had terrorised my wife and son into fleeing on Christmas Day.

I bent down to the fire, stood up again. With the poker in my right hand.

Two steps forward.

The right arm upraised.

The bird peacefully asleep.

The poker sang as it swung through the air.

Archie stirred inside a dream, alerted by the singing of the poker. It was already falling backwards from the armchair, the wings were beginning to unfold and the feet were slipping from the perch, a fraction of a second before the blow landed. The poker connected with the cormorant's shoulder, the bird was flung onto the carpet with a dull thwack and a cloud of dust, the sound of a stick against an old pillow.

Archie was awake.

I lurched after it, wielding the poker. I was shouting, but again it was the distant distorted voice which I had heard in the pub. There was the bird on the floor behind the sofa. The wing I had struck just as the cormorant had begun to fall away was out-stretched, black and tattered, smashed. I lunged forward with the poker, ready to strike. Archie scrambled away from me, dragging the broken wing and rowing along the carpet with the other. It unleashed a torrent of guttural sounds, snaked its head with the dagger-beak open. Around the room we went, drunken man and wounded bird, and the poker fell again and again on the chairs and the floor, whistled through the air and struck the table and the tree, sent the books tumbling from their shelves, lifted the dust from the cushions, brandished like the baton of an inspired conductor. I heard my voice repeating the tired old oaths. The room was filled with dust, the flailing progress of the poker. I listened wearily to the voice, the rushing of surf inside my head. There were books, Christmas cards, decorations and sherry bottles on the carpet, feathers and green shit, and everywhere the air was heavy with the cries of the cormorant. I drove it to the door and tried to stamp on the trailing wing, to pin it down and hold it still for the delivery of a fatal blow, but the bird was in the kitchen, over the cold floor and into the yard. I stood at the doorway, shivering from my exertions and the icy air from the garden, watched Archie go scuttling into the upturned crate which still lay outside the cage. With difficulty, the bird manoeuvred itself into the box and turned its head to pull in the injured wing with its beak. It burrowed far into the straw. Then it was still.

Big flakes of snow were drifting through the darkness, settling on the slates of the backyard. I looked up at the sky and down at the poker in my right hand.

The sounds in my head subsided. In my pursuit of the bird, I had forgotten something, something I could postpone no longer. Dropping the poker with a clang onto the kitchen floor, I walked straight out into the yard, to the wooden crate. I set it upright and stared into the straw. There was a little rustling movement as though the straw itself was breathing, and I could see some black feathers buried in the bedding. The snow settled on the ground and stuck for a second on the warm dampness of the straw. I straightened up, undid the zip of my trousers. I was bursting. Flipping out the worm, I waited an instant before aiming a powerful jet of piss into the crate.

At first the silence persisted. The straw hissed and fizzed under the yellow stream, a cloud of steam rose into the cold night air. And the relief . . . I thought I had never pissed with such strength, such pressure, such heat. Then the bedding began to heave. From out of the straw, Archie wriggled its head and neck, but the broken wing was trapped and the bird was only able to weave the beak in protest, gasping a few faltering croaks. I bellowed with laughter and took a step back. As the cormorant sat up in the crate, its head and neck writhing from side to side, I directed the hot piss straight into its face. There was plenty of it. It flew into the bird's eyes and ran down the sleek feathers of its throat. As Archie coughed, it swallowed the bitter juice, spat it from its beak and nostrils. The hoarse cries were cut off by the jet, it was all the bird could do to keep its head moving in and out of the spray. Until it gave up dodging, surrendered to the humiliation and remained still, its head erect, eyes and beak closed tight, while I walked round the box twice, three times, aiming the diminishing flow. Finally, when it had stopped, I summoned a number of spurts as a kind of encore. I came close and shook the droplets onto the crown of the cormorant's head, tiny yellow-green drops which trembled among the wet feathers like emeralds. Finished. There was no more. Without opening its eyes, Archie subsided into the box, disappeared among the steaming straw. A little shuffling, then silence, as though there was no cormorant at all in the depths of the white wooden crate.

I stopped laughing. The worm went into hiding.

'Archie,' I said.

The snow by now had whitened the slates of the yard.

'Archie . . . ?'

I shook the snow from my hair. Louder I said, 'Archie . . . ?' until I was kneeling in the snow at the side of the box, whispering, whispering, 'Archie . . . Archie . . . Archie . . .'

I stood up, wet and crumpled, dragged the crate into the corner of the cage. I flung down some clean straw and the remains of an old blanket. If it wanted to, the bird could crawl out and fix itself some dry bedding. I went inside, stood for a minute in the cold kitchen and watched the snow thaw from my shoes and run onto the floor.

'Archie, Archie, Archie . . .' I was whispering, but the voice grew louder and louder, became a shout as I burst into the bathroom. I vomited explosively into the bath and knelt there, retching until I thought that my chest would burst.

My forehead on the cool enamel.

The cold whiteness of the gathering snow . . .

SIX

While I was sleeping on the sofa in the living-room, the blizzard outside grew and grew and engulfed the land. It wrapped its heavy white arms around the mountains and squeezed. The forests whimpered under the pressure of the polar bear's hugging. The hills surrendered the definition of their contours, the sides of scree, the gullies thick with the skeletons of bracken, the fields strewn with boulders and scored with the tracery of the dry stone walls. All this was erased by the deadening blanket of snow. Derelict barns filled up with the blowing drifts, the spoils of abandoned quarries became white things, soft things, where before they had been black warts on the countryside. The wind forced the snow into every corner of the plantations. The trees groaned with the weight which settled until it became too much and was dislodged by the next gust of the blizzard. Then the snow gathered on the forest floor, crept among the roots and rabbit burrows, so the trees felt their grip on the ground beginning to weaken. The air rang with the splintering of branches. Tall pines, whose roots were shallow in the meagre soil of the rocky hillside, leaned in the wind and fell. Every part of the valley grew heavy with snow. It deafened the streets of every village: the streets were deaf under the whirling whiteness, gardens and houses were blinded, the striding pylons became dumb. The drifts were moulded like meringue, they grew like cobwebs against the sides of the stone walls, into the hedgerows, between roofs and chimneys, shrouding the black water of streams. No-one was outside that night. Animals sought shelter in their burrows and lairs or were huddled tightly together in the comparative warmth of the outhouses. The bear hugged. The world changed. It continued to snow long after the wind had dropped, so the drifts were reinforced. Trees sighed under the increase of their burden. All was still beneath the bearskin blanket.

And I dreamed of the blizzard.

It was purple dark in the backyard. The only light came through the window of the kitchen. I was standing amid the maelstrom of snowflakes, huge soft flakes, as big and as hectic through the air as humming birds. They beat around my head before sticking on my hair and beard. Everything was silent. In spite of the power of the wind and the whirlpool of snow, there was no sound. I stood in the yard and allowed the blizzard to envelop me. In front of me was the white wooden crate of the cormorant. It was upright, filled to the top with straw. There was no sign of movement, nothing to indicate that there was anything alive inside the crate. It could well have been a box stuffed with straw, nothing else. The snow was settling briefly on the straw and melting fast. A black and purple sky from which the snowflakes tumbled; the flakes lit up white and yellow by the single bulb in the kitchen; the shadows very dark among the tangle of fuchsia and ferns and down to where the stream must have been. Centre stage: me and the crate.

And another figure: Uncle Ian.

He stood there, as he had been at the graveside of so many family funerals: the grey melancholy face which I had never really looked at, which perhaps nobody had ever really looked at, an old-fashioned raincoat buttoned over his dark suit, sturdy legs encased in their pin-stripe, and those highly polished shoes, big and stout, with snow-poppled toe-caps. Ian was smoking a cigar. He kept it cupped inside his right hand, the blue smoke escaping from between his fingers. When I looked at him over the yard, with the crate between us, there was only the overwhelming impression of the greyness of the figure: a robust figure, the shoes, the cigar, a grey cloud where the face should be.

Still no sound. Still no movement from the white wooden crate.

Ian transferred his cigar from his right hand to his lips. The trickle of smoke was a blur in front of his face. Both of his hands went to the buttons of his raincoat. When the coat was undone, the fingers opened the flies of his pinstriped trousers. And, stepping forward a pace, Uncle Ian began to piss into the straw of the box.

A grey man, lost in blue smoke, blurred in the rising steam of urine and a chaos of snow.

I began to move. Looking down from a great height, for I had grown suddenly and viewed the scene from some distance, I watched my hands fumbling at the zip of my trousers. There was blood on my fingers, blood on the leg of my trousers. The worm appeared and shuddered at the sudden cold. A big snowflake landed on its head, sizzled and vanished. I took a forward step, joined my uncle at the side of the crate. Facing one another, we mingled our piss and steam among the blades of straw.

I woke up very soon afterwards. With a yell of horror, I found myself sitting on the sofa in the cottage living-room, trembling with nausea. For, in the dream, the straw had begun to stir under the persistent pressure of hot urine. The occupant of the bedding could no longer endure the bitter spray, but burst upwards into the cold and the snow. Out of the crate, straight into the twin jets of piss, there sprang the bright blond head of Harry.

For a long time I remained on the sofa and sat with my head in my hands. It had only been a dream. Harry was no longer in the cormorant's crate, I had rescued the boy myself with the help of Mr Knapp. That much was clear. So much of what had happened over the previous night was just a confusion in my mind. There was no distinction in my memory between dream and reality. I got up painfully and slowly, drew back the curtains, saw that it was morning. The whiteness of snow on the road and the pavements just outside the living-room was dazzling. No vehicle had passed through the village that night. The snow was flawless, the air still. In the bathroom, I rinsed my eyes and my mouth before steeling myself to clean the bath. Kneeling where I had knelt the night before, I clenched my teeth and rinsed the enamel. I sprinkled a little bleach and wiped it out with a cloth until it smelled better. There was still the business of my wounded shin to deal with; it was numb, the whole leg had stiffened, there was no pain. I went into the kitchen with the intention of finding the antiseptic and cotton wool with which to clean the gash, but stopped at the window to look into the yard. It was full of snow, not just covered as a flat field or a road might be covered, but packed with a sparkling drift, forced full of snow as a goose is forced full of grain to make its liver swell. No trace of the shrubs and bracken was left, the snow was so deep it had frozen in a lovely curving wave the width of the garden right to the top of the fence. To get to the stream, a man would need a shovel. In the corner, Archie's cage was choked with snow. It had blown through the mesh of the wire and the weight on the corrugated iron was too much, for the shelter had collapsed under the strain. I went into the living-room for my coat, came back into the kitchen and put on the green wellington boots, opened the door and stepped out.

The sky was iron-grey, heavy with more snow. For the time being, however, it had stopped snowing. I shivered and stamped my feet. Pulling on the boots, I had scraped my shin. I thought I could feel a new trickle of blood going down into my sock. There was no proper shovel to hand, but the little one I used to take in the coal for the fire was sticking up from the shallower snow by the back door. It would do. I waded into the garden until the snow was too deep and heavy to move through, then I dug with the shovel to make myself a path. Up to my thighs I stood and dug, tossing back each load of snow, extricating one booted foot from the drift and plunging forward. In time, I reached the cage. To open the doorway I had to dig deeply, right to the floor of the yard. Then I scrambled inside. Even into the furthest and best protected corner, the snow had penetrated. I continued to dig, bent double under the broken roof, and the shovel rapped on the side of the crate which was buried in the insidious drift. Working faster, I felt the sweat forming on my back. I wiped away the droplets which were beginning to cling to my glasses. Faster I dug, more hoarsely I whispered, 'Archie, Archie, Archie . . .' in the rhythm of my strokes with the shovel. 'Archie, Archie, Archie . . .' and the snow flew from my blade with each word I hissed. Until the crate was cleared. Without investigating inside, I flung down the shovel and started to drag the box backwards to the doorway of the cage. Through the deeper snow I half lifted and half dragged the white wooden box, stumbling in my clumsy boots with their filling of snow and oozing blood. Straw fell out when I lurched against the packed drift. And all the time I could hear myself coaxing the cormorant to the warmth and safety of the cottage. I whispered, I urged. 'Come on, Archie, nearly there now . . . a few more steps,

get you warm soon . . . you've been colder than this before in that
bloody estuary . . . come on, Archie . . .'

Then the way was open. I staggered through the back door
with the box in my arms and put it down on the kitchen floor.
Straightening up and throwing off my coat, I switched on the
stove, shut the door to the living-room and the door to the yard.
I would soon warm up the tiny kitchen.

The table was a shambles of debris from our Christmas dinner.
Nothing had been washed up or tidied away. There were pots
and pans with the remnants of vegetables and the encrusted
leftovers of sauces, all the plates and cutlery, glasses of different
shapes and sizes; the carcass of the turkey, more than half the
trifle, which had proved too much after the main course: the
assembled disorder of a splendid feast. Most of this I moved into
the sink and onto the draining-board, the food disappeared into
the fridge. My movements were becoming better co-ordinated,
although my head reeled in the increasing steam. When the table
was clear, I put down a couple of sheets of newspaper. Then I
turned to the crate, reaching unhesitatingly into the depths of
straw, brought out the bird and placed it on the table.

Archie was frozen solid. Its neck and wings were stiff as iron,
the broken wing folded awkwardly and showing white a splinter
of bone. There was a little pliancy in the rubbery feet, otherwise
the cormorant felt hard and brittle, as though it would shatter
into many pieces if it were dropped on the floor. I held the bird
again in my hands, looked at it this way and that. But it was frozen
in just the position which it had assumed on retreating from the
shower of urine, into its wet bedding. The neck was folded to
enable the cormorant to press its face into its breast feathers,
the beak was partly hidden under one wing. Eyes closed. One
wing snugly tucked away, the other awry. Whichever way I held
it, Archie remained frozen in sleep, a fragile relic of the cormorant.
Dead for many hours.

In my befuddled condition from a night of nightmares and
nausea, my head and tongue thick with drink, with the aching
numbness of my leg, I was unable to assess the situation clearly.
Tenderly, I held the cormorant. I saw the broken bone which
jutted from among the feathers of the wing, and I remembered

the blow I had struck there with the poker. The tiny shards of ice which had formed in the velvet plumage around Archie's face and neck and throat were stained yellow, frozen urine. Wherever the icicles remained on the bird, they were yellow and green, shot through with the bitter piss. I held the cormorant close to me, hoping perhaps to infuse some life through the warmth of my hands. But Archie was stiff beyond the powers of any warming.

I drew the table closer to the stove. When I opened the oven door, a blast of hot air filled the kitchen, steaming the window and my glasses. The snow thawed from my boots and formed a puddle on the floor. I watched the transformation of the bird. Close to the heat from the oven, lying on the newspapers on the table, Archie started to thaw. The sparklets of ice disappeared. Within all the secret channels of the cormorant's throat and deep down in the dark chambers of the breast, the ice was breaking. Between every feather, the tough primaries where the ice had grown in splinters, the down on which the ice was just a bloom, there was an easing of tension as though each quill breathed a sigh and became pliant again. The iron melted in every joint. As the newspaper turned grey with the water which dripped from the bird, Archie resumed its blackness; under the light of the kitchen bulb, in the enveloping steam, it flaunted the subtle iridescence of its plumage. There were blues and purples among the black, but above all there was green. The dead cormorant relaxed on the table in a glitter of metallic colours.

And as it thawed, it moved. I was in no state to understand these movements. Archie's head creaked and fell forward from its sleep in the feathers of the breast. The head slid over the newspapers, the beak opened, and the room was touched with the smell of eels. Archie's neck uncurled, just as the heads of bracken uncurl under warm sunlight. With a click, the good wing sprang away from the body and began to spread across the table. The broken wing remained still. The entire body seemed to grow. It leaned to one side and stretched luxuriantly, like a man awakening from a satisfying sleep. And with every movement, I willed the bird to blink an eye and look around. The eyes stayed shut. I stroked the cormorant's head and dried off the drops of water with a towel, patting the bird gently and whispering all the time, 'Wake up, Archie, you're warm now . . . soon get you dry again . . .' But, when Archie's body had melted, it lay still. There were no more twitches of feathers or yawns of the sea-smell from that beak. I was beginning to see, among the steam of the kitchen and the vanishing shreds of my nightmares, that the cormorant was dead.

That was when Ann came in. I was standing very still by the kitchen table, in my shirt sleeves and wellington boots. The bird was stretched on the wet papers. She was suddenly there beside me. Her nose wrinkled at the smell. But she squeezed my arm for a second before going past me to the back door. In a moment, as I remained still and silent, she had thrown open the door and turned off the oven. She came back to me, linked one arm around mine and put her hand on my stomach. The steam was thinning, billowing into the yard. She pressed herself against me, felt how cold and wet I was with sweat and steam. I stood still and stared at the cormorant. It was all clear to her.

'Archie's dead,' she said.

I looked down at her. She had her coat and her boots on for crossing the snow-covered street. Her hair shone. She smelled of toothpaste.

'Yes,' I said. 'The snow drifted into the cage, the roof collapsed.'

'Oh . . .'

There was a long silence.

'Let's put it outside, shall we?' she whispered, tightening her grip on my arm. 'We can't do anything else now.'

I was thawing. More familiar pains were returning to my body: my head ached from the sherry and the beer, there was a strain in my chest after the exertions of vomiting. And the shin had started to throb again. 'Have you come back?' I kissed her forehead. 'Where's Harry?'

'He's all right with Mrs Knapp for a while. Now take the bird out.' She added, 'Take the bird out. And yes, I've come back.'

I lifted the limp body of the cormorant from the table, put it inside the white wooden crate and covered it with straw. I took it through the kitchen door, set it down for the time being in the shallower snow I had cleared in the yard.

An iron-grey sky. There would be more snow soon.

Ann knew when she had the ascendancy, and she exploited it in the knowledge that it might not always be hers. The cormorant was gone. There was a void. She led me into the living-room. While she prepared boiling water, antiseptic and bandages in the kitchen, I had some minutes to work on the debris of my night alone: the blankets, bottles and glasses, books and Christmas cards which were scattered across the floor, the gouts of shit which was the cormorant's signature. I moved slowly about the room, bending to gather a handful of pine needles or a few black feathers. I replaced the books, took the blankets upstairs, collected the evidence of my drinking bout. Ann sat me down on the sofa, gently drew off my boots and socks, wriggled me out of my trousers. She had a basin of steaming water. With cotton wool, she sponged away the dried blood which had congealed all over my shin and ankle, down to my foot, in between my toes. It all came off. I lay back with my eyes closed. The gash itself was revealed. With tweezers, she lifted the flap of skin, having melted the scab with plenty of hot water, saw the whiteness of the bone beneath, applied the antiseptic directly into the wound. She ignored my shouted oath: there had been a surfeit of those in the previous twenty-four hours, they no longer meant anything. Now the shin was clean, she bandaged it with sweet-smelling gauze and crepe. She kissed my foot then ran upstairs for some socks and jeans.

'There's a brave boy. That didn't hurt, did it?'

I was not allowed to rest. Taking me by the hand, Ann tugged me into the kitchen again. The back door was still open. When I went to close it, she just said, 'Leave it, let's have some more air in here.' And we tackled the Christmas dinner dishes. Hardly a word was spoken. There was too much bustle in the little room for words. I had no time to think of the pain in my foot or the absence of Archie. She thrust into my hands a succession of plates and bowls and cutlery, saucepans and gravy boats. My arms immersed in soapy water, I cleaned the dishes. The window steamed up, I took off my spectacles, it was snug even with the door open to the yard. We turned in the confined space and brushed together, hip against hip, her hair across my face, her breasts loose and heavy on my arm. Our eyes met. She did not smile, but she winked the wink she had always saved for me in the reverential hush of a staff meeting or across the bedlam of the playground.

'Not finished yet . . .'

There was no flicker of a smile.

'Light the fire, dust and hoover the living-room. I'll inspect it in a quarter of an hour, so make it good. And I'll do the bathroom.'

I fetched coal and wood, baffled for a moment as to the whereabouts of the shovel. Ann didn't see me go out to the cage, tip-toeing in my slippers through the snow and past the abandoned crate. I heard her muttering in the bathroom: perhaps my efforts with the bleach had not been thorough enough to erase all the evidence of my sickness. I felt better moving around, breathing deeply when I knelt at the hearth, busy with newspapers and kindling wood. A tall, rather surprised-looking flame rose among the nest of coal. Disguised under the drone of the hoover, I attempted a line or two of song, and there was Ann at the doorway, watching me and listening. She nearly smiled. In the fragile silence which succeeded the machine, she checked the carpet for pine needles, ran a finger along the mantelpiece.

'That's better,' she said to the quivering flame. 'The place was a real mess after yesterday.'

She smiled.

The cottage was newly cleaned. Harry was in good hands for a short while. Under a growing drift of snow, Archie was freezing stiff for a second time. The best and safest place to be for the two of us that morning was bed. Ann led me up the stairs and into our bedroom. The bed was untouched: that was almost the saddest thing, that nobody, no loving couple had shared the bed on Christmas night. For an hour I was her invalid, a bruised and damaged man who needed her care, her warmth. She slowly undressed me, careful to avoid contact with the fresh dressing on my leg, and she tucked me up in bed. Then she undressed. She would let me do nothing. I was her man. She was going to love me while I lay there, I could simply rest and be quiet. Lifting the sheets, she slipped into the bed. With every part of her body she made love to me, applying herself to me as though she were a priceless lotion with which my wounded body should be anointed. As I lay still, she coated me, she oiled me, she bathed me with herself, until I knew again each silken surface and scented shadow and had them imprinted on my skin. And when I turned to her, to put my hands on her, she only said, 'No . . .', breathing the word into my hair. Before I slept, however, she rolled on top of me, so that her breasts felt heavy on my chest, and she asked me suddenly: 'Tell me, my love, did you kill the cormorant?'

I looked past her, at the ceiling. I remembered more of the previous evening, in disjointed sequences, like random flashes of old newsreel. Someone had helped me back from the pub . . . all those drinks which were bought for me. Why had Archie been released into the cottage? Who had put the poker in my hand?

I thought for a minute and answered.

'I don't know . . .'

Ann turned her head, looked away, as though she wanted to allow me more leeway for my reply. But I repeated, with absolute, unshakeable certainty, 'I don't know.'

Then we slept, still and silent, enfolded in each other's limbs, oblivious to the tumbling snow.

When I awoke, I was alone, cold and frightened. But the space beside me was still warm. Sitting up, I strained every muscle to hear or feel some movement in the cottage. A surge of panic overtook me, my head was full of suffocating fog, and I sprang from the bed. Before I could struggle into my clothes, there was the sound of the front door opening and closing, the scuffling of footsteps on the mat. It was Ann, back again from across the street, with Harry. When I tumbled down the stairs in a disarray of untidy clothes, the boy beamed from his mother's arms and flung out his hands towards me. His little face was cold and ruddy after the short journey. When I kissed him, it was delicious, like the first electric sip from an ice-laden gin and tonic. Together we fell onto the sofa, amid squeals of giggling, more tickling and the tingle of kisses.

'Don't take his coat off.' It was Ann's teacher voice. 'Let's all go out in the snow. It's so lovely and clean out there. Get your boots on . . .'

I was soon wrapped up in my jacket and scarf and gloves. Ann fixed Harry's hood so that his face was tightly framed with fur.

She put on a hat whose flaps folded over her ears and buttoned under her chin. I felt the fleeting regret which sent a tremor through my belly: that her throat, with its marble shadows and the quivering of a hot pulse, should be covered up. I would undo those buttons myself when we came in from the snow, and see that the throat was still warm.

So, to the cleansing by snow . . .

The three of us, encased in our winter clothing, staggered out of the front door. In the middle of the road, the snow was shallowest where there was nothing against which the drifts could form. We went crunching through the silent village. I had Harry in my arms. Ann's hand was snuggled in my pocket, like a hibernating vole. Passing the pub, we heard the cries of the persistent revellers, the few who had walked from their houses in the village. I grimaced at the smells of beer and smoke. Ann noticed and squeezed my arm. 'Naughty man,' she said. The bench on which I had been sitting in the previous night's drizzle was almost buried in the snow. We continued by, turning through a gap in the stone wall of the roadside and wading into the drifted snow of the woodland. I put Harry down. The child was light enough to negotiate the snow without sinking more than a few inches, and, with an expression torn between horror and delight, he made his first tentative steps over the smooth crust. When he fell, his tiny gloved hands vanished into the drift and his face was forced on the snow. He rolled over, spitting. There were crystals in the fur of his hood and spangled in his lashes. Harry was going to cry, but he looked up at our expectant faces and laughed instead. Ann's hands flew to his cheeks to brush away the flakes, but he fought himself upright and continued his exploration. In his boots, mittens and padded suit, the child strutted up and down the sugary hills of snow. More than a dozen yards away, he would turn to see us, to check that we were included in his brand new universe. Yes, there we were, sitting together on the cold dry boulders of the wall.

'Hey, young Titus!' I shouted. 'Don't go too far or I'll be forced to send your mother out looking for you!'

Harry spun around at the voice, grinned and clapped his hands. The snow flew from his gloves and settled like tinsel on his red cheeks.

Onwards through the plantation. When we reached the top of the hillside, we could see all the way along the valley and glimpse the grey turrets of Caernarfon castle. Somehow, the whiteness gave an unusual clarity to the day, in spite of the leaden sky. As the road wound into the distance, full of snow but clearly distinguished by its lining of walls and hedges, it snaked between the hills, appearing and disappearing. Trees and telegraph-poles stuck up like the bristles of a hedgehog. All things which were not woolly with snow were black or grey: there were no colours in the landscape. I set Harry down from his vantage point on my shoulders, and he discovered the cones and needles of the fir trees, digging his mittens deeply into the snow. He snarled at the cold which soaked his fingers. Then we waded over the ridge, with the village just below us. A spiral of grey smoke was rising from the chimney of our cottage, all the roofs were white, the row of houses was the decoration on a Christmas cake. Further along the ridge, we looked down into the gardens, simply squares of a uniform whiteness, very clean. Everything was clean. We could hear the rumbling of the stream, but the water was shrouded in its tunnels and chambers of ice. The air grew suddenly colder with the advancing of the afternoon, the sky began to frown. Gripping me by the hand, Ann led the way down an opening in the forest, where the snow was not so deep between the black trees. Darkness soaked into the day, soaked and spread like the blooming of ink on blotting paper; it seemed to issue from the trees, was exhaled from the sky, from the ground itself, seeping upwards through the blanket of snow. And before we could reach the road again, we saw the streetlights flicker: blossoms of orange flowers in a monochrome garden. Half-past four. Without speaking, we made our crunching way past the pub, watched our own footsteps set off into the woods. Harry too was silent. The village was cast in gold by the lamps on the pavements. Every sound was muffled.

The cottage windows gazed at the passers-by, wide-eyed and tearful. The sky went blue-black with a snap, and the stars were there, as brittle and bright as broken glass.

Home again.

I set about refuelling the fire with two logs of horse chestnut, thinking too about the flaps of Ann's hat, the heat of her throat after the cold walk. I began to undo the buttons of Harry's coat. But the day was still Ann's, she maintained the advantage.

'Leave his coat,' she said to me, as I knelt with the child on the hearth-rug. 'We're going out for a bit longer yet.'

Harry had resumed his mesmerised scrutiny of the flames which trembled around the white wood. He stared into the fire as though he and the yellow tongues of light were the only living things in the room.

'Into the backyard,' she continued. 'We're still not completely clean.'

Her expression silenced the beginnings of my questions.

'Is there a drop of petrol in that spare can? Get it from the car . . .'

The kitchen light flooded the backyard with brightness as it fell on the covering of snow. There was no sign that anyone had been out there that day. My work with the coal shovel had been obliterated. One corner of the crate was visible. Ann carried Harry outside and put him down in the snow. When I came back with the petrol can from the van, she was shovelling the snow from around the cormorant's crate. Harry blinked in the light, rather dazed by the cold and the surrounding darkness and the spectacle of his mother's digging in the drifts. She stood back with the shovel in her hand, her face aglow with the effort, very lovely in the snow-filled garden. Once more, the crate was exposed. I put down the can, stepped forward and shifted the crate away from the wall and into the centre of the clearing. She glanced at the can.

'I'll do it,' she said briskly, and carried on without waiting for an answer.

'Matches . . .' I said, ducking back into the kitchen.

Through the window I watched her, the tumbling of golden fuel from the mouth of the can onto the white wooden box. Outside, I took the can from her. I poured the petrol into the straw. Shuddering convulsively, I shut out the dazzling image of the previous night's dream. Harry was watching from the kitchen door, a bland smile forming on his mouth. The straw was silent and still. I did not reach down into it.

'Pick the boy up. Keep well away.'

So, to the cleansing by fire.

I struck a match, allowed it to flare up between my cupped hands, and tossed it into the crate. It went out. Again. Again it fizzled in the wet straw. But, the third time, the fire began.

One moment the yard was white in the glare of the kitchen light, and then it flamed into a furnace of reds and golds and yellows. The fuel in the crate went up in a mighty whoosh of fire. Blades of straw flew out with the torrent of golden sparks. The box burned with a silver fire of its own, the flames running from bottom to top and fighting like a nest of lizards. The flimsy wood buckled and split. Out spilled the straw, a crackling ant-hill of writhing heat. The crate lost its shape, became a ball of flames as the sharp lines of wood were consumed. I watched with my hand to my forehead as a shield against the glare, the fingers of my other hand locked in Ann's. She also stared, and held fast to Harry. He was impassive at first, as though the explosion of colour after the blacks and whites of the forest was an unspeakable blasphemy to which there was no appropriate reaction. But when the straw fell out and the box was no longer a box but a thing alive with fire, he wailed and convulsed against his mother's breast. Both his hands were flung towards the blaze. His eyes bulged and he shouted in a language of strange words. He wrestled like a weasel in her arms. The purple sky and the bitterness of the air retreated from the flames, but Harry lunged towards them. The fire was his. He wanted it, he raged for it.

What happened then seemed to last for ever, but was probably over within a minute. The garden was rocked by the explosion of the petrol can which was ignited by the trickle of burning straw. In that second, white fire came spewing across the yard towards us, rolling over the ground and over our feet like water. We leapt away, but the garden was full of the shrieks of the flames, there was silver fire in our eyes and in our ears. The air contracted around us. I remember only the hurtling noise of the explosion and the brilliance of light. And a vision of Harry, escaping from his mother's arms.

He dropped to the ground, cat-like among the blaze. With a shout, he sprang forward, across the pools of shallow fire, over the dancing puddles of spilled petrol, and immersed himself in the flames of the white wooden crate. Engulfed by the fire, the little figure was tearing and rummaging at the remaining panels of the box. As I waded after him, he tossed handfuls of burning straw into the air, plunged into the bottom of the crate. Into the fire I followed him, but he was a shrinking shape among the heat. There were tongues of flame on my trousers, sparks in my hair and beard. Involuntarily, I retreated in a series of ungainly leaps. My hectic hands beat at my clothes. Beside me, Ann was immobile, staring with dead eyes into the searing blaze. Again I went into the fire, again my body was beaten back, my hands a-flutter at the pain of burning skin. We could only watch, mesmerised into apathy. As the flames diminished, the blackness of the garden grew around us. There came a sigh from the shrinking lake of fire, there was no definition of shapes amid the lessening blaze. No crate, no cormorant, only the incandescent figure of a little boy. He was changing, in colour and outline, as he continued to scrabble into the seat of the fire. In the centre of the orb of billowing flame, the child too was shrivelling, molten, blackened, issuing twisted plumes of smoke as he folded and collapsed like an exhausted candle. He crumpled into the hottest remaining core of the blaze, his figure replaced by a mushrooming pall of vapour, pungent with the stench of scorched flesh. The air crackled, fizzled and hissed with the explosion of many blisters. Gaping like the mouth of a sightless fish, the fire sucked. It fell inwards on itself. Its muffled implosion was the belch of a glutton.

Ann sank to the ground. Unconscious, asleep, she fled the horror of the funeral pyre, safer, perhaps, in a world of dreams.

For myself, uncertain of what I should have been doing, utterly dazed and dazzled by the fire, I trod stupidly among the embers. I kicked away a few relics. My feet shuffled through blackened wood and charred cloth. They turned over the blistered bones of bird and boy. I found the shovel in my hands once more. From the corners of the garden I brought snow and sprinkled it on the remains. They sizzled. Smoke rose where the flames had been. Working faster, I came again and again with shovelfuls of snow, my eyes blurred with tears and the bitterness of ashes. All the air was heavy with the reek of burning.

Until the blackness of the fire was hidden with a mantle of immaculate white.

EPILOGUE

With the coming of the thaw, the garden was emptied of snow. The stream was black and vicious with the melting of ice. I sat in the cottage and shuddered at the shrieking of the gales. In January and February, the mountains had groaned under the weight of snow, each night had stalked up the valley and suffocated the hillside with its chaotic darkness, until the rains came and the days were grey with the soaking they received. The country drowned. The fields sucked at the legs of the livestock. Mud, more rain, a quagmire of mists and drizzle: forever the sound of water, from the sky, from the roaring gullies, from the roadsides, and flying from every blackened branch and blade of grass. A landscape of greyness and water. The winter spent itself in March by assaulting the windows of the cottage and throwing soot down the chimney. A few slates flew off the roof. Water crept under the doors. The building dug its claws into the land, gripped and waited. The relics of winter faded.

Nothing remained of the cormorant, not a speck of ash or the grain of a singed feather. Harry was gone. Ann was still unconscious when they came to take her from me; her destination, in a welter of flashing blue lights and powerful sirens, was never clearly explained. Alone in the cottage, I stared into the fire, gripped the arms of my chair and flinched at the tumult of storms. I waited.

But, with the end of March, once more the sun appeared, splashing a little watery colour onto the mountain-sides. Like a great big dog which has come running up the beach after its frolic in the surf, the mountains shook themselves and sent a final shower of rainbow spray into the valleys. Then they relaxed. A little steam rose from their backs under the touch of the sun. Still the stream bellowed. But there was a prickling of green on the hedgerows, sparks of yellow in the grass, the daffodils and primroses.

It was spring.

The sunshine beckoned me into the garden. I would stride over the slates and sniff the air, stand and watch the hectic water of the stream. Alone in the garden. Until the gulls came . . .

They descended on me like the snow which had choked the garden at Christmas. I sniffed the tingling air and braced myself with my feet apart, simply stared into the sky and waited. No sounds, no cries or whispers.

But the gulls came.

At first a solitary bird came skimming over the plantation and peered down at the garden. Its laughter rang hollow against the hillsides. Until another gull appeared, and another, and the hysterical mirth increased. I stood still, my face upturned. And my sky became a blizzard of the whirling white birds. They dived towards me, their throats gulping with the effort of screams. Their wings made the air quiver. A patter of droppings rained on the slated path and settled like tears on my cheeks. I never raised my hands to wipe the tears away: I let them trickle to the corners of my mouth.

Then, when the turmoil was too much and in my head there was nothing but the snowstorm of gulls, I could dismiss them. I simply dropped the butt of my cigar and ground it out with my heel on the slates of the garden. The birds wheeled upwards. They wept a little and were gone.

The snows had vanished, for the time being. In the garden it was spring again.

Spring again, for the time being.